THE SEA WITHDREW

FOUNTAIN OF YOUTH TRILOGY
BOOK TWO

MIRANDA LEVI

THE SEA WITHDREW

Miranda Levi

EMILY DICKINSON POEM WAS PUBLISHED BEFORE JANUARY 1, 1928 AND IS IN THE PUBLIC DOMAIN WORLDWIDE BECAUSE THE AUTHOR DIED AT LEAST 100 YEARS AGO. – ACQUIRED FROM HTTPS://EN.WIKISOURCE.ORG/WIKI/I_STARTED_EARLY_%E2%80%94_ TOOK_MY_DOG_%E2%80%94

COVER ART BY RQPUBLISHING.COM

IG: MIRANDALEVI_AUTHOR

TIKTOK: MIRANDALEVI_AUTHOR

HTTPS://MIRANDALEVI.COM/

HTTPS://RQPUBLISHING.COM/

ISBN: 978-1-961714-09-0

ALSO BY MIRANDA LEVI

From A Youth A Fountain Did Flow

The Sea Withdrew

A Tear In Time

Mo(ther) Na(ture)

In Orion's Hands

MIRANDA LEVI

Additional Books by Rainbow Quartz Publishing

Lorelai Hamilton

Find Your Bliss

Teenage Witch's Grimoire

Tarot Reflection Journal

Tarot Refection Journal Coloring The Tarot

The Eclectic Witch's Grimoire

Dream Journal

Teenage Tarot

Tarot Tales and Magic Spells

Arcane In Verse

Isla Watts

A Fairy Bad Day

Surprise! You're a Vampire

Gorgeous, Gorgeous, Gorgons

Mork The Handsome Orc

Adopted By Werewolves

Bite Me If You Can

That's The Spirit!

Rose Dawson's Book Journals

My Time With The Fairies

Enchanted Escapades

Enchanted Escapades

Dewey Decimal Diaries

Siren's Songbook

Pride and Prejudice

Bibliophile's Bounty

Book of Books Journal

Pages & Passages Reading Journal

Bookworm's Companion Reading Journal & Tracker

This book is for my mom.

The queen of strength and sass.
You've turned challenges into triumphs.
Thanks for being the bold ink in the pages of my life.

Love, M

MIRANDA LEVI

I STARTED EARLY—TOOK MY DOG—

I started Early — Took my Dog —
And visited the Sea —
The Mermaids in the Basement
Came out to look at me —

And Frigates — in the Upper Floor
Extended Hempen Hands —
Presuming Me to be a Mouse —
Aground — upon the Sands —

But no Man moved Me — till the Tide
Went past my simple Shoe —
And past my Apron — and my Belt —
And past my Bodice — too —

And made as He would eat me up —

As wholly as a Dew
Upon a Dandelion's Sleeve —
And then — I started — too —

And He — He followed — close behind —
I felt his Silver Heel
Upon my Ankle — Then my Shoes
Would overflow with Pearl —

Until We met the Solid Town —
No One He seemed to know —
And bowing — with a Mighty look —
At me — The Sea withdrew —

—Emily Dickinson, 1862

BOOK TWO

PART ONE

THE PAST

"The only difference between the saint and the sinner is that every saint has a past, and every sinner has a future."

Oscar Wilde

CHAPTER 1

SCARLET

3 MONTHS EARLIER

All the air is sucked out of the room, my lungs compress in on themselves right before everything spins. Just as quickly as we enter the portal, we pop out the other side.

"I will never get used to that," I say, holding my chest as if I could push air back into my body.

"Come on, we need to keep moving," Zig says. "This way."

We move at a slow jog, trying not to draw attention to ourselves, but somehow we fail. Two young adults in a strange city, bumping shoulders, bags, and signs as we hurry through the streets.

I'm not even sure where we are—a bustling city, for one. New York?

I feel a stranger's eyes on me, watching us whoosh by with hardly an apology in the wind.

We must keep moving.

All we can do is keep moving.

"Where are we going? We don't have a plan, Zig. We need a plan." I attempt to squash the building anxiety in my chest, the little voice that says this is all going to end in a dark place.

That no one will walk away from it alive.

That Zig will die.

That I will die.

It doesn't work.

"While logically, I know my ring is untraceable, we have to be careful. I don't trust The Circle not to have its own methods for tracing the untraceable, you know? I still can't shake this feeling we're being watched. I don't know. I don't want to freak you out, Scarlet, but it feels like you're being watched," Zig says.

A chill starts at the top of my head and spreads down my back to my fingertips. I shiver.

"There's a good chance we're okay, Scar; it's a big world. I just need to be sure," Zig says. "I have to be sure."

Zig's eyes are soft, and it breaks my heart. He's not ready for this. For what this means. I don't think he understands the full ramifications of what we just did.

"Nothing is okay. I am not okay. My world just keeps imploding, and now I've dragged you along," the words tumble out of me. I hold back a sob.

I should have left Zig behind.

I should have found the courage to leave him.

"There's no point in dwelling on the past. What's done is

done," Zig says. "I'm here, and you won't get rid of me that easily."

He pauses long enough to wipe away a tear that's found my cheek.

"Give me your ring," I say and hold out my hand.

Zig stops in his tracks. "No."

"Give me your ring. You shouldn't be here, Zig. I shouldn't have let you come."

"No," he says more firmly.

"Zig."

"Scarlet, I'm not leaving you," he says.

"And if you die? I couldn't live with myself," my voice breaks.

"It wouldn't be the first time. Besides that, it's my choice. You don't get to make my choice for me. You don't get to protect me this way."

"I—" I start but lose my words. I would hate him for making a choice like this for me. For not letting me choose my own destiny. "Fine," I capitulate. "But we need a plan. I'm not going to blindly follow you."

Zig drags me off the main street and around a corner. "Do you trust me?"

I close my eyes. I don't want to answer him. If I answer him, it will only lead to something dumb.

Risky.

Stupid.

The truth is, I do. "Yes. But—"

"Okay, this way."

Reluctantly, I follow close behind him, and we pop down an alley. It's a dead end, but Zig continues with purpose.

The area is deserted, and I'm suddenly thankful for it. Zig moves his hands down a wall until he finds what he's looking for.

"Come here," he says.

I reach for his hand and take a deep breath, holding it. The world shrinks around me, my lungs compress, and when I open my eyes, we've come out the other side of the portal.

"Blend," Zig says in a hushed whisper.

It only takes me a couple of minutes to realize we're in France. I listen and overhear folks talking outside a café. Not that I speak it, but I know enough random French words to put two and two together.

Zig has slowed his pace to a saunter, and I match him. He reaches for my hand, and I let him take it.

"I'm hungry and tired," I say, biting back the sudden tears that threaten to fall. "Can we find somewhere to rest for the night?" I need time.

Time to process and wrap my head around all of it. Plus, it's late here.

Zig thinks momentarily and pulls out his wallet, counting the cash on hand. "Neither Azeltha nor I considered money. If we use my card, we'll be traced. We could pull it out now, but we'd have to keep moving."

"Do we have enough for the night? We could pull out the rest and ditch the cards later. Are they really going to try tracking you through your bank account?" I ask.

"I don't know. We don't have a lot of tech magic. Honestly, magic usually stops working when it comes to technology for most witches. Marcus is a rare one who's been quite successful with tech."

"Marcus isn't going to hunt us down," I say definitively.

Zig nods. "You're probably right."

"Can't you just magic some money or let folks think we paid?"

Zig's brow furrows. "You know it doesn't work like that for me."

"I don't. Tell me, how does it work?"

"Later? I'm feeling weary myself." Zig runs a hand through his hair.

"So, we can rest then? Worry about money tomorrow?" I ask.

Zig smiles, and for the briefest moment, I'm lost in his eyes. I forget all about the world, about Dagon, about leaving Mundi. I let all my worries melt away.

ZIG BOOKS US A ROOM AT A MODEST HOTEL WHILE I GRAB DINNER at a local restaurant. At first, he insists on never leaving my side, but after I remind him that I'm more than capable of taking care of myself, he eases.

Something about ripping the hearts of men out with my bare hands. I don't want to do it, but I have.

When I get back to the hotel, Zig is waiting outside.

Stiff.

I hold up my hand, showing off the spoils I've procured.

Zig doesn't seem to notice.

"You okay?" I ask.

"Hmm? Yes, I'm perfect," he says.

"I've got dinner. Did you get a room?"

He absently checks his pockets and pulls out a small envelope. "It seems so, room 104."

I take the key from him and find our room. Zig moves alongside me, taller somehow.

"Are you sure you're okay?" I ask.

"Perfectly fine," he says.

Perfectly fine? I shake away his words and lock the door behind us.

I feel the veil of control slipping off me. A tightness moves in my chest, up to my throat, choking out any words I might have tried to find.

My hands are trembling.

Zig comes from nowhere and takes the bag of food out of them. He sets it down and then leads me to one of the beds.

The tears spill, and a sob rocks my body. Zig puts an arm around me. He doesn't say anything, but he holds me. He combs through my hair with his fingers, and I lay in his lap, letting every horrible thought and fear leave my body through tears.

When I can breathe again, the tears that fall do so on their own accord, however gently.

Zig kisses me.

It's soft.

He holds me all night, whispering that things will be okay.

Zig whispers over and over, "Everything will be okay."

I don't believe him.

But I sleep.

CHAPTER 2

MARCUS

"Marcus? Ho trovato quei libri di cui mi chiedevi," Professor Bertelli says.

"My Italian is rough. May we speak in English or Spanish?" I ask.

"Si. Thanks for coming out here. I've found the texts you were asking about," Professor Bertelli says.

"May we speak privately?" I ask.

"Si. This way," he leads, and I follow.

While Rome is a breathtaking city, Sapienza University is nothing special—well, aside from the professors, that is. The history department is world-renowned. This history department is breathtaking. I'm betting Scarlet's life on it.

It's been three months, and I feel further from saving her than the day she left with Zig.

Professor Bertelli turns down a hall and into a dimly lit room. "Right this way," he says.

When I step into the space, it's wall-to-wall books. From a cursory glance, ancient texts sit alongside more modern college textbooks.

"I don't know if I can wait any longer," I say, wringing my hands together. "I'm dying to know what you've found on Dagon."

"It wasn't easy at first. There is very little written documentation about him," he says.

"For months now, I've found nearly nothing on my own. Whatever you found has to be more than all my combined months of searching."

Professor Bertelli waves a finger at me. "To put it plainly, Dagon was a god. He ruled over the sea. The worship of Dagon dates back to the third millennium BCE in Mesopotamia."

"He's not a prince of hell?"

"Well, that's more complicated. Short answer: no. Not originally, at least. He was, however, an important deity in the city of Mari during the second millennium BCE. Dagon was also worshiped into the late Bronze Age and the Iron Age. He was associated, in particular, with the Philistines. He was their primary deity."

My mind explodes with questions. Was he actually a god or only the manifestation of a demon? Is this helpful for tracking Scarlet? The sea? What came first, the demon or the god? I bet he was a fish. The sea?

The smell of bacon penetrates my thoughts. The professor is telling me the truth. There's honesty in the air, so I don't interrupt with my parade of questions.

"The worship of Dagon continued into the Hellenistic and Roman periods, with temples dedicated to him being built in various parts of the ancient world," Professor Bertelli says, shuffling the books and spreading them out. He points to another one. "In Hebrew mythology, Dagon was the Jewish fertility god who was half-man and half-fish."

"Half-man and half-fish. As in, he was a mermaid?" I ask. It's way better than a fish. Let the bastard be a mermaid.

Professor Bertelli shrugs. "He was depicted in a way that present-day scholars might describe as a mermaid. But he was bigger than that. He was the god of the sea, agriculture, fertility, and fish. There are instances when he is fully man and others where he is fully fish. But yes, in most depictions, he is a mermaid-like figure."

"A mermaid," I say wistfully.

"With the rise of Christianity and the spread of Islam, the worship of Dagon and other ancient deities declined and eventually disappeared altogether," Professor Bertelli says.

"I'm trying to make the connections and wrap my head around all of this," I say. "When did he become a prince of hell? Or am I misunderstanding, and he's both? Neither? Is it two different beings?"

"Well, to put it simply, the ancient gods were rewritten to suit the needs of more powerful religions, much the same way pagan holidays were rewritten to meet the needs of those in power. How do you squash out beliefs? Change them, rewrite history, and eventually, the new narrative becomes gospel after a couple of generations. The first time we see Dagon written in the Judeo-Christian texts was between 630 and 540 BCE."

"So, if I understand correctly, he wasn't always a prince of hell. He was a mermaid first?"

The professor chuckles. "Mostly, yes. The winners of wars write history, Sir Marcus. From what I can tell, Dagon was revered for his greatness, his good. But now," he trails off.

"But now, he's predominantly known for his darkness."

"Si."

"He's a demon."

"Even the word demon has only been used in its current iteration since 1400 AD," he says.

"I don't understand," I say. "What did it mean before then?"

"The word demon referred to anything of the occult. Even angels were referred to as demons. There were never any connotations of evil or malevolence. The Greek word *eudaimonia* literally translates to good spiritedness or happiness."

"But why?" I ask, confused.

"Fear."

I shake my head. "I still don't understand."

Professor Bertelli sighs. "All it took was a united shift of opinion from the many. The new powers eyed cities with pagan statuary. The word demon came to represent malevolent and deeply evil beings."

"Someone wanted to gain power, so they changed the meaning of all things happy in one religion to all things bad in another?" I say in a poor attempt at summation.

Professor Bertelli gives me a half-smile. "You are not so young?"

"Do we know when the word demon was first used as we know it now?"

"Specifically, it was the Septuagint translation of the Hebrew Bible into Greek."

"So Dagon is both a god of the oceans and a demon?"

"Si."

"Dagon is a mermaid."

"Si."

CHAPTER 3

DAGON

I was bred from rule breakers. It should come as no surprise when I tell you that death was not the end. For me, it has always been a new beginning.

Death comes for me now.

Perhaps, in some ways, she perpetually does. I have danced with Death for so long I've forgotten the terms of our agreement. Maybe it was one life in exchange for another. Or was it my life in exchange for war?

It feels so unimportant now.

Scarlet beams at me, and I see the smiles of all those who came before her. Her face and the color of her eyes change, but her smile is always the same.

Ishara was the first.

When she was taken from me, I vowed to burn this earth to the ground. Wash away humanity's sin the way they tried to wash me away. Turn earth into ocean. Expand my dominion until those who forsook me are no more. Let them all burn.

"She will die at your hands until the end of time."

I took his last breath for even conceiving of such a curse. It was deliberately slow and as painful as I could make it. I sank his vessels and raised the ocean over his home, drowning them all.

Ishara was my way of being.

She was my reason.

Kind. Loving. Vibrant and full of life. Ishara was everything.

In every way possible, she still is.

She is mine.

If I can't have her as my own, no one else will get the chance. Ishara gave herself to me freely.

One day, she will remember who she is. I can wait until then. I've waited three eternities thus far.

There have been moments when Ishara remembers. But our time is short-lived, and I am cursed to lose her over and over again. I live for those moments in between the darkness.

Scarlet and I walk.

Our time nears.

I think of all the ways she trusts this body.

"I thought we could walk around the park first? If you keep your shield up?" Scarlet's gold-flecked eyes search my own.

Does she see him or me? Does she see the monster or the man?

Do I care?

I spin thoughts of her in my mind—of her soft skin, of blood pumping just under the surface. How easy it would be to break her.

Maim her.

Taste her.

Possess her.

Worship her.

In this chest, animals roar and stampede. This heart beats uncontrolled, even by me. I muster a smile and hold out my hand for hers. She intertwines her fingers with mine.

No.

Mine.

"Zig?" Her voice is soft, a question teeters at the edge of her lips.

"Hmm?" I breathe.

"You okay?"

"Perfect," I say.

Scarlet is mine.

Chapter 4

Scarlet

Zig's words echo in my mind, "I had no choice. It was me, or it was her."

I don't know what to believe. I keep replaying the scene in my head over and over again.

"Hmm? Attacks?" Zig said, absent from the conversation.

"Demons? Meat suits, you know, the whole reason we're on the lam?" I said, laying the sarcasm on thick. Maybe all he needed was a whack to his ego?

I wanted to scream, *Where are you? Where did you go? Come back to me.*

But I refrained.

Stupid.

"I'm sorry, my mind is elsewhere," Zig rubbed his eyes.

"I know. You've been somewhere else for months," I said, wringing my hands in frustration.

"I guess that ring Marcus gave you is doing its job. It was supposed to protect you, stave off your scent. Right?" Zig's words carried a tone of distaste.

After everything he shared about Marcus being his brother, I thought Zig was missing him, too.

Have I been wrong this whole time?

How can Zig hold anything but love for his brother?

"I suppose so," are the only words I can conjure. They don't scrape the surface of all the things I feel.

The pathway is lined with wildflowers. I'm too busy noticing their varied shades at first to look up and notice the woman standing in the middle of the path.

"We've been looking for you everywhere, Sir," the woman says.

Her words draw my attention away from the flowers. Her eyes are what set my blood to ice.

Before I can say or do anything, Zig attacks. He breaks her neck in two quick movements.

Her eyes, black as the darkest night, are full of surprise.

This meat suit wasn't expecting an attack. She didn't fight back.

"What did you do?" I drop to my knees at her side. I check her pulse. "She's gone."

"I had no choice. It was me, or it was her," Zig looks at me unapologetically. "We have to move."

Zig's words play in my mind but no longer align with his actions.

"We could have saved her," I say.

"We can't save everyone. If I have to choose you or them, I choose you."

Zig leads me away. I glance back at the body of the girl and wonder what her family will think. Who she's left behind, and for what?

If it's me or them, I choose them.

CHAPTER 5

DAGON

Despite being single-handedly capable of protecting Scarlet from anyone except myself, she doesn't know that I can do that. She doesn't know that I could light the world on fire and ravage it from end to end without leaving a single mark on her ivory skin.

Scarlet only needs protection from me.

So instead, we're careful.

We still spend time in old libraries and bookstores. Scarlet hunts for information and anything that might provide her a reason.

I could give her reason.

Only, she's not ready to hear it.

I've tried distracting her with carefully placed books and documents, but she continuously overlooks them.

I've tried beating it into her in past lives, but that proved to be the wrong method as well.

I shall try patience this time.

Try being the operative word.

While Scarlet is off decoding the secrets of her afterlife, I attempt a cunning and quiet infiltration of the magical variety.

Being in this body has its benefits. Scarlet's trust is number one.

However, there are unexpected limitations. I've fractured my abilities.

Or perhaps this body malfunctions.

I'm not broken.

I ignore the voice of my host.

Hosts aren't usually this bothersome. This one refuses to let go. I even promised a painless death, but it's done nothing to alleviate its futile hold on such a shred of existence.

My magic is—limited.

Time in this vessel is limited too.

Once a god among men, I was feared by all as one of the greatest demons in the underworld. Now, I'm reduced to a lowly meat suit stuck in a debauched pairing.

Not that I'd tell a soul.

If anyone saw me like this, knew what I'd become—

Stuck.

I'd be ruined.

Scarlet would run, and I'd be forced to kill her.

Again.

The others in the netherworld would hunt me. It was a close call the other day, walking in the park. How dare anyone talk to me in public?

They got what they deserved.

A kindness, really. Slow and painful would have been my preference.

I don't think Scarlet believes me. Skepticism rolls off her in waves of putrid disgust.

"Do you remember the first day we met?" Scarlet asks.

A flash of a long wooden table, deep purple curtains, and long raven hair.

Hazel eyes.

This false memory knots itself with my own. Ishara standing at the edge of a cliff overlooking the ocean. Her hair danced in the wind. I could have stayed in that moment forever.

"Of course I do," I say. "I could never erase you from my mind, even if I tried."

No, you can't have it.

I'll take what I want from you.

Scarlet's cheeks pinken. "I wish my memory was as good as yours."

"Oh?"

"Was it Kara's backyard or Azeltha's kitchen table?" Scarlet asks.

Hers is the only face I see.

"It was at the kitchen table. There were others with us, but yours was the only face I could see," I say.

Scarlet absently strokes my arm. "That's right."

"You really don't remember?" I ask.

"It's not that. It's more like the veil of grief was so heavy, it all blurs a bit."

I wonder briefly if I've passed her test. "Are you okay, darling?"

It's ever so brief, but I'm certain Scarlet cringed.

From me.

From her Zig.

Not Zig.

Yes, Zig, I say firmly to the host in my head.

You.

She cringed at you.

Scarlet searches my eyes.

Zig's eyes.

She reaches for my cheek and grazes it softly. "Have your eyes always been such a dark shade of blue?" Scarlet asks.

"I suppose I don't look at them often enough to tell you," I say. "But I've been told they change colors based on my mood or the time of day."

"You've never mentioned it," Scarlet whispers.

"Didn't seem relevant," I say.

"Considering what we know about the demon underbelly, it seems extremely relevant." The windows to Scarlet's soul are but slants, her soft eyebrows furrowed.

"I didn't know I was under suspicion, my dear," I move a thumb across one brow, and she relaxes.

"Mmm," Scarlet moans as I move my fingers over her other, working my skillful touch into a light head massage.

"I guess I didn't want to bring up some other girl from my past when you're the only one that has ever mattered. I didn't mean to upset you," I say.

Scarlet pats my leg. "As long as you don't stop with that," she generalizes the space where my hands are. "I'll let it slide this time."

I chuckle, and I can feel her smile.

All is well in this corner of the world.

Chapter 6

Marcus

"You've found misguided comfort in mermaids," Azeltha says.

I glance up from the stack of books sprawled out on my desk. I've grown more accustomed to Azeltha popping into my space since Scarlet's departure.

"I never said—"

"The room smells of sprinkles and rainbows, boy," Azeltha says.

"I am not happy," I say.

Until three or four months ago, Abuela was the only other telepath I'd spent time with. I've known two or three, but we're a rare breed. Abuela rarely reads me, or at least she doesn't call me out on it when she does.

Azeltha, however, is a different story. Being around her seems to push my boundaries to a ten every single time. I can never lie or have a thought she won't point out.

"You know as well as I that just because I smell happy doesn't mean you are happy. It means you're finding pleasure in something. By looking over your shoulder, I can only assume your comfort is from mermaids. You should never find comfort in a mermaid, Marcus," Azeltha says, sitting gingerly on a chair beside me. "Why the sudden interest in the love children of Loki?"

"Are they?" I say with great enthusiasm.

"No."

I scoff. That would have been wicked.

"What? I might be old, but I'm still funny," Azeltha smiles. "Tell me what you have here?"

"I met with a professor in Rome about Dagon. While I couldn't take the books he had, I managed to acquire some photocopies. With a little spellwork, I've been able to recreate most of the text," I say, scooting one of the books over to her.

"This is some delightful magic, Marcus," Azeltha says, flipping through the book. "Most folks forget about the beauty in this world. This is some of my favorite kind of magic. The recreation is nearly flawless."

"Nearly," I say, pointing out a missing page I couldn't fill in one of the books.

"So, what have we learned about Dagon today?" Azeltha asks.

"He wasn't always a demon," I say.

Azeltha's eyes grow large.

"Prior to the spread of Christianity, he was a sea god. A mermaid."

I try to read Azeltha's face, but she gives nothing away. No smells, no emotions.

Nothing.

I continue, "From what I've read so far, he was a benevolent deity, and as much as I'd like to deny it, he wasn't always a demon. I just don't know if I understand."

Azeltha clicks her tongue and offers no more.

"The professor said the winners of wars write history," I say.

"He's not wrong," Azeltha says, breaking the silence she let hang for far too long.

"Are you saying that Dagon was a mermaid?" I ask.

Azeltha tilts her head, measuring me.

"What aren't you saying?" I ask, impatience gnawing at me. "I thought we were in this together. How can I understand if everyone keeps things from me? Fighting blind isn't going to do anyone any good. Not me. Not Scarlet. Not Zig."

Azeltha straightens in her chair and clears her throat. "You're right. Anything necessary to protect her."

The air thickens, with the faintest hint of hot Cheetos. Sadness and guilt move through Azeltha.

"I only want to understand. I can't exactly talk to Abuela about this," I say. "She's been acting as if nothing has happened since Zig's departure. Whenever I bring up Scarlet, she cuts me off and adds more busy work to my plate. As if I don't have enough going on already. As if it's just another day, and the past year never happened."

"Kara loves you. She's only trying to protect you," Azeltha tsks.

"I don't need protection from my Abuela. I need honesty," my words come out hotter than I intended.

"Okay. I need you to understand something first," Azeltha says.

I nod. "Anything."

"This world is more than you know it to be."

"I mean, I guessed that. Mermaids were never on my radar before. I'd heard stories, but I assumed it was all bogus and myth at best," I say.

"It's more than that," she says.

"I'm listening."

"The fabric of our existence hinges on belief. Mermaids are real because millions of little boys and girls believe they are," Azeltha explains.

I shake my head. "You're saying that if I believe in something enough, it becomes real?"

"No, I'm saying when the belief of a thing becomes so prevalent that it's woven into the fabric of society, it becomes real," Azeltha says.

The saltiness of bacon sends a chill down my back. Bacon means truth.

"Mermaids are not just folklore?" I ask.

"Mermaids are not just folklore," she says.

"Dagon is a demon because people believe him to be one," I say, still struggling to believe the words as I speak them.

"I'd always had my suspicions that Dagon wasn't always a demon. But I couldn't prove it," Azeltha says. "I knew there was more to him."

"This doesn't prove anything. It's only text," I say, unwilling to accept her truths.

"In a similar manner to the adaptation of holidays, ancient gods underwent reinterpretation to align with more influential religious beliefs," Azeltha says.

"That's exactly what the professor said. If you're telling me you knew this the whole time…" I grit my teeth, pushing down my annoyance.

Azeltha sighs. "I do not know everything, Marcus. But I will say this: mermaids are not to be trifled with." Azeltha stands. "You'd do well to remember that."

"Not even if Dagon is one?" I ask.

"Dagon is a demon." Azeltha tilts her head at me.

"And if he's a mermaid as well?"

"Then he's even more dangerous than we believed. He would have a siren's song. He could sing you to your death before you knew what was happening."

I close my eyes, letting her words wash over me.

"Mermaids can do grand things if they choose, but they are capable of equally grand malevolence. They are wicked creatures," Azeltha says.

"Every time I think I understand this life, the world spins," I say.

"You are young, Bisnieto," Azeltha says.

Anger washes over me, and I tamp it down. Lashing out will do me no good.

"I think perhaps it's time you spent a while with Joe," Azeltha says.

"Why? No one on the council takes me seriously. They see

me as a threat. Sleeping with the enemy," I say, then immediately regret my words. I take a deep breath. "I mean, not *sleeping* with. We never—were just friends."

Azeltha smiles. "Because Joe can teach you things. And he misses Zig. It might be good for both of you."

"Ahhh," I say.

"Don't be quick to judge. I'll set something up. Until then, keep reading. You have a lot to learn. I want updates," Azeltha says before disappearing as quickly as she arrived.

CHAPTER 7

SCARLET

Zig is a meat suit.

It's the only explanation. It's not just the color of his eyes; it's the words that drip from his snaky tongue.

The real Zig would know precisely how we met: Kara's kitchen table during a council meeting.

Zig never went to Azeltha's. The real Zig would never confuse the two. Never in a million years. Never in my life.

Never.

Yes, I set him up to fail.

But Zig would have never failed.

So, it was never a setup.

He's a meat suit.

Zig isn't dead, but he might as well be. There's no one here to help me exorcise this demon. I don't know how to do it alone.

I can't do it alone.

I'm afraid to think about who it is.

Afraid I already know the answer.

But when?

Was it recent? Or has Zig been gone since the beginning?

The most embarrassing part—if some piece of Zig is in there, he knows I've failed him.

How long have I gone oblivious to the demon sleeping in my bed?

I push away the thoughts, unable to let them linger on the darkest parts of my soul.

I could fight it. I could kill whatever is living inside Zig, but I'd kill Zig, too.

So, it's out of the question.

Not even fathomable.

Think, Scarlet, think.

I have no way of contacting Marcus. Even if I did, pulling him into the middle of more of my mistakes is also out of the question.

Azeltha is equally unreachable.

Silently screaming, I blow out a breath.

I miss Mom.

My mind spins around my limited options. I have no cash or way of knowing where safe houses would be. I can't rely on The Circle's network. I can't exactly blend in here. And I don't have the ability to portal on my own.

Fuck.

My eyes prick, threatening tears.

Deep breath, Scarlet.

You are Scarlet Singer. You have lived a thousand lives before. You have been through worse, and you will survive this.

You will live to see another horrific sacrifice.

This is not the end.

This is—tears spill down my cheeks.

I grab my bag, already packed for whatever the supernatural world throws at us. I don't have much to my name, but it's all inside this backpack. I peek into Zig's things and find a couple of twenties. I pocket them. It's not much. He must have the rest on him. I'll join one of those odd-job apps. I'd need a phone for that, though. Maybe I can nick one.

Gods above, I never thought I'd be stealing cash for survival.

It's not Zig.

It's not stealing if it's not Zig.

I slip on my hoodie and tuck my hair inside it. Zig is grabbing us dinner, so it's now or never. My window is closing.

I don't know where we are. I'd guess one of the Germanic countries, but I can't even say for sure.

Deep breath. I open the door, half expecting Zig to be standing there.

He's not.

I leave as quietly as possible and take a left onto the street. I read somewhere that most people take a right when fleeing. It probably has something to do with most of the population being right-handed. It's dark and raining—all to my advantage.

The night is filled with the whooshing of cars and the

quiet chatter of folks walking on the sidewalk. There are restaurants filled with people enjoying fancy dinners and wine, living their normal lives.

I hang another left and then a right on the next block, keeping my face out of the light. Trying to put as much space between myself and Zig.

Between myself and the meat suit.

I duck into a crowded bar, making my way out the back door and onto the street. There are stairs that lead to a subway station, and I follow them. The train is pulling in as I approach. The screeching sets my teeth on edge. I manage to slip onto the train and into a seat. There are instructions, but I don't know what they say.

Doesn't matter as long as this thing puts distance between me and it.

Two minutes pass before the train leaves the station.

For the first time in days, my lungs fill easily.

I wipe water droplets off my hoodie, nestle my bag into my lap, and just breathe.

I am alone.

There is no one to save me.

No one to run to.

I can do this.

"Did you think you could run?" a voice says.

My stomach turns to ice. All the air is thrust out of my body. I look up to find Zig sitting across from me.

Not Zig.

A meat suit.

CHAPTER 8

ZIG

Only in the darkness do my thoughts have room to breathe.

He extinguishes every moment I assert.

My mind is not safe.

My memories are for the taking.

Scarlet.

Oh, Scarlet.

She finally understands.

Too late.

Dagon.

Dagon.

Dagon.

CHAPTER 9

GEMMA

6 MONTHS EARLIER

"The Fountain is afraid of needles. Who would have guessed?" I say flatly.

"What will you do with the sample?" Scarlet asks.

Like I have time to explain all the ins and outs of my work to a kid who's only trying to distract herself. "I'll start by analyzing it. Blood can say a lot, all by itself. Your DNA will tell a specific story that only yours can. No two are alike," I say.

"And you need a thousand vials to learn this?"

My gods above, so dramatic. "Eight is not a thousand."

"Might as well be."

"I thought you were supposed to be wise or, at a minimum, above anything as tedious as a blood draw, Scarlet," I say, raising one brow.

"Sure. I'll be whatever you want me to be because that's how it works, right?" Scarlet says.

I don't have it in me to deal with her adolescent antics. The world is bigger than you, Scarlet. It's bigger than all of us.

Gods above, if you only knew. With the tiniest glimpse behind the mirror, you'd freak and run from this place quicker than you can spell magic. Blood draws are the least of your problems.

Chains, cages, and what's behind the void—those are better things to fear, little Fountain.

Of course, I don't say this.

Can't upset the Fountain.

Kara has only made that clear a hundred times.

"It's my understanding that being the best you is the only way to be. I could be mistaken, though. I know I'm not nearly hip enough," I say, grabbing another vial and swapping out the full one for an empty one.

"I'm an orphaned seventeen-year-old. I'm as wise as my memories of lives cut much too short in a time that has little implication on today's society. I can't remember what Kelby did to help The Circle, and no one else seems to be the wiser about it. I miss my mom. I've been in the care of The Circle for months, and I feel as small and insignificant as the first day Kara found me," Scarlet takes a breath. "I'm sorry I haven't found the time to ratio-nalize blood draws in my brain. I've been a little preoccupied."

After filling the last vial, I remove the needle from Scarlet's arm and place a cotton ball on the entry point. I grab a bandage.

Scarlet removes the cotton. "Don't bother," she says.

The small injection point heals itself. It happens so quickly that I'm not sure I remember it clearly.

I hand Scarlet a glass of juice. "You should drink this."

"Anything else?" Scarlet asks.

All I can do is shake my head no.

She leaves, and I'm left needing more answers.

I stand at the gates of hell, feeling my soul being stretched to the limitations of its being.

I know this is a bad decision.

The absolute worst.

Bloody hell.

What am I doing?

Walking to the center of a wolf's den with raw flesh strapped to my naked body.

It's suicide.

The door creaks open to the cabin before I've had a chance to step up to it. There's nothing but darkness within.

"What do you want?" says a voice from the ether.

A shiver runs down my back.

"It wasn't hard to deduce who the infamous Z was," I say.

The door opens all the way, and I hesitate before walking in. Raw meat and a lioness equate to suicide. Every muscle in my body wants to bolt.

It's dark, and instead of being greeted by warmth, I am bombarded with a cold front. Ice infiltrates every nerve in my body.

"I will only repeat myself once," says the voice. "What do you want?"

A lump moves through my stomach, knotting itself. I stand a little taller and set my shoulders.

Show no weakness.

"I'm here to discuss the Fountain," I say.

She moves into the light. For the first time in two decades, I lock eyes with the monster who took everything from me.

"There's nothing to discuss," she says, turning her back to me.

The lump slowly moves to my chest, choking me along the way. "I remember the quiet whispers when no one was around. The threats. The death."

Her face gives nothing away.

Another breath, "You may have silenced every uttered word from hushed lips, but you missed a few of us. You missed me."

Her body tenses, and I brace myself for a lashing that never comes.

"I know about Kelby—and her predecessors." The words don't finish leaving my mouth before she's nose to nose with me.

"Mors labia fontis parabolam loquuntur," she says.

Her harsh words penetrate my soul. Magic wrapping its way around my throat.

Into my cerebral cortex.

My being.

Every inch of my existence.

"Speak one word of the Fountain, and you shall suffer the same fate as the others," she curses.

"Azeltha," her name a miserable sigh, barely choked out.

"Your kind is the reason she was hunted," Azeltha spits her words. "How dare you come into my home."

"I only wanted to—" I start, but she cuts me off, my words strangled from my lips.

"You only wanted to stir up the past. To hold knowledge over my head? You don't deserve the air you're breathing after the way you've benefited from her."

"I didn't make those decisions," I say.

"But you ameliorated from it. You all did."

I know she's right.

I can't deny the truth.

"Speak of the Fountain to anyone, and I will personally cut your tongue out and jar it up as a trophy. I will curse your soul to live and die like hers."

"I'm sorry," my words are a whimper.

"It's decades too late for apologies," Azeltha says.

"I'm sorry," I say, reaching into my pockets for the vials of blood.

"Leave."

"But, I—"

"I won't say it twice," Azeltha's words are sharp.

I feel her magic wrap tighter around my throat, making it difficult to breathe.

The door swings open, and I drop the vials on the ground. Blood splatters across the floor.

I leave without looking back.

The lump forms a pit in my stomach as her curse wraps its tendrils around my throat, embedding their tentacles into my spinal cortex.

Scarlet Singer—flames lick the insides of my veins.

Mors labia fontis parabolam loquuntur.

Only death's lips speak the parable of the Fountain.

That murderous bitch cursed me.

CHAPTER 10

MAGS

In a dark and faceless distance, I hear my name on the lips of a human. They carve sacrificial symbols into the earth, dripping blood of belief and life, providing me with a doorway back.

Time is not linear, but it is limited.

Heeding the call of curiosity, I walk the path where the light meets darkness—where belief in something meets the void of forgotten dreams.

The fog of destiny is thick.

We all have a part to play.

Light.

Dark.

It's all meaningless without reason.

We all have our reasons.

No two are the same.

Long ago, I had a reason.

I had hope.

I had love.

Now, all I have is revenge.

I let the pull seep into my being. The sacrifice soaks into the threads of my life force.

The crossover is never long but always painful.

Born into life through agony. Flames licking every inch of my essence while drowning, gasping for air I know will never come.

The pain never subsides until I take a body. I move with thought from one destination to the next—an apparition in the night, drifting on air.

The memory strikes me before the aroma registers. We are drawn to our own. Bodies change, but the memories remain. A meadow at sunrise, slightly damp from the night, and a hint of pennyroyal wafts in the air, drawing me in.

The bodies are always connected.

There are rules. It's never as absent of purpose as the humans would have you believe.

We are always connected.

It wouldn't work otherwise.

The thinner the connection, the shorter the stay.

Bodies degrade quickly when Death enters them.

The stronger the connection, the more extended the stay.

It's the only way Death remains away.

I can feel the call of sacrifice on the horizon—the burning of herbs, the smell of blood, my name on the lips of those with a wish.

All in due time.

The aroma grows stronger, and I follow.

Death is but a gamble.

One I intend on winning.

Her body seeps memories into the air, pennyroyal as sweet as the day I first breathed it in. As she takes her next breath, I slip inside.

Gone from the void, I settle into my new shell. I suck in air and remind this heart how to beat again.

CHAPTER 11

SCARLET

"There's no point in partaking in this charade anymore," I say. "If you're going to kill me, just do it already. Stop playing with me before the slaughter. It's just fucking rude."

"When did you get such a saucy mouth?" the Zig suit says.

"Dare I ask?" I say.

"You dare," their voice is a slow rumble that methodically rolls down my body.

My voice catches before I find courage. "W-who are you?"

"You've known me since the beginning of time."

I shake his words away. "No—No. That's not even possible."

"Okay, then tell me, Scarlet," the Zig suit shifts forward. "What do you want to know?"

"How do I get off this train?" I stand, feeling the subway slow.

Zig stands.

Not Zig.

I'm feeling nihilistic.

At the next stop, I exit the train, tripping over myself and the platform, but I don't run.

It follows me.

We walk up the stairs from the subway to the city side by side.

"You're not going to run?" the Zig suit asks.

"What would be the point?" I say, trying to keep the wobble from my voice.

"I didn't expect this approach. You're disappointing me," it says.

"Is that all it takes?"

He looks at me through familiar eyes. A flood of memories moves through me, and I can hardly keep the tears at bay. "Is he still in there?" I ask.

"Your precious Zig?" it says.

I nod.

"For now," it blinks but doesn't look away.

"Until you use his body up, too worn out to save." I spit my words.

For a moment, I consider running. But if he's going to kill me, there's nothing I can do but die. I can't save Zig from his fate any more than I can run from mine.

"Where did all this hostility come from?" it says. "I've been quite good to you."

"This is good?" I laugh. "I'd hate to see your definition of bad."

"Perhaps we can avoid that road a little longer," it says.

"Perhaps you get out of Zig's body and leave me alone?"

His smile rips through my chest.

Zig's smile.

"It's not that simple," it says.

"Of course it is. I know you can move into any body you'd like or return to whatever spawning location you spewed from." I throw up my hands. "Forget all about me. Let me live my life in peace."

"How long will you avoid my eyes?" it asks.

"How long do you plan on seeing through Zig's?" I say.

"You haven't minded thus far," it says.

"What gives you that impression? Was it all the lies I blindly believed?" I say.

"It wasn't all lies. And you are not blind," it says. "I, for one, know you can see just fine."

I think back over the last few months, but I don't want to know.

Not yet.

Zig holds a door open for me. I follow him inside before I have time to register where we are. Immediately, I knock over a stand filled with postcards and keychains. Zig catches it, righting the whole ordeal before I get my bearings.

Not Zig.

"You done destroying the place?" he asks.

"You're one to talk," I snark.

"Can I help you?" asks a man behind the counter of this little tourist trap.

Zig's eyes flash black.

"Right this way, sir," the clerk says with a knowing grin.

There's no turning back now. Just follow the demon possessing the body of the boy I—I can't even finish the thought.

What if it was never him?

Oh god.

What if it was never him?

"The second shelf on the right, and you'll be walking out to the morning," the clerk turns around and leaves.

"This is outside The Circle's network, isn't it?" I ask.

He strolls to the second shelf and grabs a trinket. Zig's hand reaches for my own.

"What's your name?" I say, having found the slightest shred of courage.

He clasps my hand with his own and smiles. "Dagon."

The room spins. All the air is sucked from my lungs.

I'm going to puke.

Abruptly, everything is calm and still.

I don't open my eyes.

Let it be a dream.

Let it all be a nightmare.

I peek one eye open.

"Still Dagon," he says.

Suddenly, I'm bent over, dry heaving the bile in my stomach.

Dagon moves toward me, and I stumble backward. "Who did you think I was?" he asks, curious.

I can't bring myself to admit that a small part of me knew. "Don't touch me," I say, wiping my mouth.

I can't kill Zig.

I can't make myself kill Zig.

I won't do it.

"I think we have some things to discuss. I thought we could go somewhere private since Pandora's proverbial box has been opened. There's no point in lumbering around other humans unnecessarily. I'd hate for any more accidents to happen," Dagon says.

"It's not an accident if you do something with intent," I say, wishing my words could slap him.

"That's not really here nor there," Dagon waves a hand.

"Why are you playing with me?" I say. "Just kill me and get it over with."

Dagon shifts, uncomfortable, but his face doesn't give anything away. He turns from me and walks away.

A beat passes before I resolve to catch up.

I'm out of my ever-living mind.

"Where are we going?" I ask.

"I'm hungry," Dagon says.

"You're hungry?" I repeat and stop walking. "The demon eats?"

"Must feed the human. You coming?" Dagon asks.

Marcus would be so angry with me. But he's not here, and I only have my conscience to lead me.

I trail behind Dagon, alert for whatever trap I'm walking

into. If he's going to kill me, I'll take things into my own hands. I don't want to leave Zig helpless.

All I can do is try.

We arrive at an outdoor restaurant. We must be somewhere in Europe. I just can't quite pinpoint where.

Romania?

That's a wild guess, but I've always wanted to visit, and the area seems familiar somehow. I'd bet money on it.

Reluctantly, I take a seat across from Dagon.

The waiter smiles. "Știi ce ți-ar plăcea sau ai nevoie de un meniu?"

I don't understand him.

Dagon matches the waiter's grin and speaks flawless Romanian. "Vă rog să ne aduceți o comandă de sarmale, mici, pomana porcului și cozonac. Asortați-l cu o sticlă de vin. Mulțumesc."

The waiter looks at me. "A bottle of water, please?"

"Da, desigur," the waiter says before walking away.

We sit in silence, waiting.

Waiting for food.

For death.

Waiting for whatever comes next.

"I have a proposition for you," Dagon says.

A surge of fire ignites in my belly.

One of the first questions Kara ever asked me was if I'd made a deal with a demon. Traded something for years of my life. She was looking for a reason to explain my mother's murder.

There isn't a proposition in the world that could be worth her life. I can't imagine there's one worth mine.

Basically, this can't end well.

I say nothing.

"I know you want this body back to its original form. Host and all," Dagon's words are a rumble that sends shivers down my spine.

I sit up straighter.

"I'm willing to part ways with it," he starts.

My heart leaps with hope.

"If you're willing to be mine," he finishes.

A false hope. "Be yours?" At first, I didn't realize I'd spoken.

"Yes."

I'm shaking. Not just my hands, but my entire body trembles. "I'm my own person."

"Scarlet," Dagon says incredulously.

I close my eyes. "I'm my own person," I say more firmly.

He says nothing.

"It can't be that simple," I say.

"It rarely is," Dagon sits back in his chair as the waiter delivers a bottle of wine and water. He proceeds to pour us each a glass.

"Do I have a choice?" I ask.

"You always have a choice, dear one. Even when they're not your first."

"What happens to Zig?"

"When I leave this body, that will be up to him." Dagon fingers the rim of his wine glass.

"When will you leave his body?" My voice betrays me, refusing to be more than a whisper.

"That will be up to you."

I take a calming breath and dig deep to find strength. "I have conditions."

"I expect nothing less, my dear," Dagon says.

"I'm not your dear," I say.

"Not yet."

CHAPTER 12

DAGON

S carlet is a rainbow in a world plastered with grey. A glimmer of unadulterated pleasure pushes through my deadened soul.

"What are your terms?" Scarlet asks.

"You've barely touched your food," I say, taking a bite of mici, a savory BBQ sausage-like dish.

"I'm not hungry," Scarlet pushes her plate away petulantly.

A smile plays on my lips. "You haven't eaten since breakfast. You can't pretend with me."

"I said I'm not hungry," she grits her teeth, anger pulsing off her in white-capped rage.

"First condition, you must take care of your body. Feed it when it requires sustenance, and rest it when it requires recovery," I say.

Scarlet rolls her eyes.

I slam my fist on the table.

Scarlet startles and grabs her fork. She stabs a piece of meat and shoves it into her mouth.

"I'm not poisoning you like The Circle would have. All I want to do is nourish you," I say.

"You want more than that. So, stop playing games already," Scarlet takes a swig of her wine. Her face contorts, and she coughs.

I pass her a glass of water.

She takes it eagerly. "Thank you."

"Much to your disappointment, I want to be honest with you," I say.

I almost mean it.

"Honest?" Scarlet says, laughing. "That's real rich coming from you. Please, what do you know about honesty?"

"More than you give me credit for," I say. There was a time when my honesty would have never been questioned.

I sigh.

In time, I know Scarlet will understand.

She is resistant, but this, too, will pass.

"It's so easy to hate you," Scarlet stabs another piece of meat on her plate. She smells it this time, satisfied, and plops it into her mouth.

"And here I am trying to give you reasons to adore me," I say.

"You're not funny," she says with her mouth full.

"That's not what you said last week," I remind her.

Silence.

Her eyes narrow.

"Condition number two," I say. "After I abandon this host in favor of more appreciable lodgings, you stay with me." I hold up a hand to stop her from interrupting me. "Nothing like that required."

Scarlet's already narrowed eyes become mere slits. Her face is cold and unwavering. "Then tell me what it's like. Tell me what staying with you entails."

I lick my lips. Is it too much to hope?

"It means that when the choice presents itself for you to flee with The Circle, instead, you choose me. You stay with me."

"What makes you think they'll come?" she asks.

"They'll come. They always come," I say.

Scarlet pushes the food around her plate with her fork. "And if I don't? If I decide to flee instead?" Scarlet asks, her body rigid.

"Then this host is mine until this heart beats its last, and your friend goes to a place I've never been, beyond the confinements of this world." I pick up my glass of wine and sip.

A shiver moves through Scarlet's body. Her hand shakes. "I want my own conditions," she says.

I raise a brow, genuinely surprised by her bluntness. "What, pray tell, are you asking for?"

Scarlet finds my eyes. "Honesty."

"Honesty?" I try not to laugh.

"Yes, honesty. You claim to be oh so honest with me. I want to know you can't lie to me," Scarlet says. "I need to know that you're being one hundred percent honest. And if you're not, there must be a consequence."

It's not like I've been overly dishonest.

But unadulterated honesty?

Forced honesty?

With Scarlet?

"Anything else?" I say, pondering her request.

"You never get to possess me again. My body is my own," her voice carries a slight wobble, though I would never call her on it.

"Let me see if I have it correct. In exchange for leaving this host alive, you require a truth spell between us, and I must give up the ability to possess your body. After which, you'll be mine?"

"Zig lives?" she asks.

"For as long as you keep your oath."

"Complete honesty and my body remains unpossessed?"

"For as long as you keep your oath."

Scarlet closes her eyes. She lets out a breath and puts her hand out.

"This will require more than a verbal agreement," I grin. "We'll need a blood oath at dusk for this sort of magic."

"A blood oath?" Scarlet's voice goes up an octave. I can't decide if it's because of who she is or who I am.

"Eat. We'll need a few supplies," I say. "Eat, and don't tell me you're not hungry. You'll need your strength."

"For the blood oath?"

"For what's to come."

CHAPTER 13

ZIG

When I scream, can you see me beyond the monster?

I'm not worth your life.

Let him have me.

Free yourself.

Run.

CHAPTER 14

SCARLET

Supplies. Let me guess: the blood of a firstborn child, the death of a savior, and a heart ripped from a once-beating chest.

Ugh.

I don't know if I should believe him or throw the whole table over, screaming and clawing his eyes out till my dying breath.

Anxiety has found its way into every cell of my body.

Once upon a time, I was Scarlet Singer. Now, I'm a fractured offshoot of that girl.

Rage and anxiety mingle until I'm not sure which thoughts are my own and which were born of me.

Of my body.

All I can do is protect the ones I love.

"Eat, and don't tell me you're not hungry. You'll need your strength."

Strength? "For the blood oath?" I ask, terrified of his answer.

"For what's to come."

I may regret this decision for the rest of my endless, relentless, anguished lives.

One day, someone is going to ask me why. Why did you make a blood oath with a demon? Why did you sacrifice so much for so little? I'm going to need a good answer when that day comes.

My stomach gurgles.

That day is not today.

I grab my fork and eat.

DAGON AND I ARE WALKING DOWN A STREET. THE SUN HAS another hour before reaching dusk here. Although, I suppose it doesn't matter where we are. We can find dusk all over the globe.

I'm not ready for dusk to come just yet.

"What supplies do we need?" I ask, hoping beyond all hope that it's not overtly morbid.

"Don't worry your pretty little head about it," Dagon says.

I want to rip his still-beating heart from his chest and put an end to it once and for all.

But I can't.

So I stop and turn back in the other direction.

"Where do you think you're going?" Dagon's voice is a growl.

"Honesty." I spin around. "You don't get to belittle me or walk around like you're some kind of fucking god. You're not better than me."

Dagon's eye twitches. I wonder briefly if my words have any effect on him.

Unlikely.

"We need a turtle, wisdom, love, respect, bravery, honesty, humility, truth, and blood to complete the spell," Dagon says nonchalantly.

"That makes no sense," I say.

"I never said it would," Dagon says. "You asked for honesty."

"So, explain it to me then."

"Can we walk and talk?" Dagon points down the street.

What choice do I have? He didn't call me on my bluff, so I walk toward him.

"A truth spell is rarely an easy one. What you've asked of me requires a deeper understanding of magic. Lucky for you, I'm old and versed in such trivial things," Dagon says.

I let his words wash over me while we walk. "Does anyone have to die?"

"We all must die. Death and taxes, as they say. Unless you're filthy rich. Then it's just death," Dagon says deadpan.

"For this spell to work," I clarify. He knows what I mean. He's just finding pleasure in toying with me.

"Yes. Someone or something must die for this spell to work."

"Okay," I gulp.

I'm not sure what else to say.

I'm not innocent.

I've murdered.

I've held a beating heart in its last moments before ripping it from the body of my enemy.

It doesn't make this any easier.

More challenging in some ways.

At least I can say I didn't know my blood could exorcise demons from human bodies when I killed those people.

Forgiving the woman in the mirror is the mountain. Killing for my own self-needs. I'm not ready to move that mountain just yet.

"Pick a few of those daffodils," Dagon points to the bright yellow flowers growing in front of a store.

I pick five and drop them carefully into my bag, hoping no one sees me plucking their garden.

We keep walking.

"Where are we going to find a turtle?" I ask.

"I know a place." Dagon leads me down an alley and up a fire escape. We climb to the fourth platform. He feels for something on the wall with one hand, and with the other, he reaches for my hand. "Hold your breath."

The world spins and flips, knocking all the air out of my lungs. When it stops moving, I let go of Dagon.

A nearby sign reads *Turtle and Tortoise Sanctuary of London*.

"We're not going to—" I trail off.

"Do you want the long or the short answer?" Dagon says.

"The short answer," I say, unable to stomach the potentiality of the long answer.

"No."

A momentary reprieve from this nightmare. Killing helpless turtles isn't what I signed up for.

Dagon leads me deeper into the reserve. We walk the path, and I stay behind a fence when he hops over it.

On the other side are turtles. Many of them are in a large open area with lots of grass. For a moment, I'm tempted to hop the fence, too. I want to pet one and see what they're all about. I've never seen a turtle up close.

But I refrain.

Dagon pulls something out of his pocket that glints in the light.

A knife?

He leans down.

My stomach lurches.

Dagon holds a turtle in one hand and a knife in the other.

I watch in horror, holding my breath, unable to move or do anything.

He's whispering something, but I can't make out what he says. Dagon slides the knife along the backside of the turtle's shell. When he's finished, he sets the turtle back on its way and places the scrapings into a tiny jar he's pulled out of his pocket.

I tilt my head.

"I told you no, but you assumed I was lying," Dagon says.

I have no reply.

"Maybe after this forsaken spell, you'll give me a chance."

"Unlikely," I roll my eyes.

We leave the turtle refuge almost as quickly as we arrived. Taking another portal.

This time, when I open my eyes, we're somewhere dark. Across the street from us is a biker bar. A dozen motorcycles are lined out front, a handful of trucks, and a couple of beat-up piecemeal cars. A single lamppost lights the parking lot of the dingy, reddish building.

To our right is a sign that reads *3.2 Miles* with a symbol indicating gas. There's road in all directions. I realize we're standing in the middle of a four-way intersection.

"Where are we?" I ask.

"At a crossroads," Dagon says. "I'm here to collect a debt."

"Are you—"

Dagon cuts me off, "Don't ask me a question you're not ready to have the answer to," he says. "You can't have it both ways. You can wait here if you prefer. This won't take long."

"I don't prefer," I say, regretting the words as soon as they leave my lips.

"So be it." Dagon leads the way.

Inside, the bar is dingy, tinted red, and covered in a thick coat of dust. Sour beer wafts in the air. An unfamiliar country song plays on a jukebox in the corner.

A woman hovers over it, feeding coins in exchange for more honky-tonk.

A man with a Pabst beer saunters by me and spits into his can. He looks me up and down and whistles.

I want to crawl out of my skin.

Dagon pulls out a stool at the bar. "What can I get you?" the bartender asks.

I don't sit.

Dagon doesn't say anything. His eyes flash black before turning back to their ocean blue. The bartender stumbles backward.

"Now, now," Dagon says. "Don't make a scene, Jeffery."

"It's been a long time," the bartender, Jeffery, says with a twang.

"Ten years, to be exact," Dagon says.

"I thought maybe we could come to a new agreement," Jeffery says. He's wearing a plaid overshirt, jeans, and a backward baseball cap. "Let me get you a drink on the house." Jeffery reaches for the bottle of top-shelf whiskey.

Dagon sits long enough to enjoy the double whiskey shot on the rocks.

"I know it looks like I haven't done much with what I requested, but I'm just getting the ball rolling. I'm planning an expansion here, and my girl, she's expecting," Jeffery says hurriedly. "Look, man, ten years isn't as much time as I thought it would be. I'm not saying I ain't grateful or anything. Because I am. I just think I could offer you more. We could come to another agreement."

"Let's talk," Dagon says, standing and pushing in his barstool.

Jeffery comes around, a second drink in hand.

Dagon puts his arm around him. "I'm sure we can come to an understanding," Dagon says.

Jeffery downs the drink he brought over for Dagon and breathes a sigh of relief. "Thanks, I have some ideas," Jeffery says.

The two walk away, buddy-buddy until they're out the backdoor of the bar.

I think of the sleazy men inside the bar and follow. As they say, sometimes the easier choice is the demon you know.

"I was thinking," Jeffery starts, "What about five more years? I know people. Powerful people."

Their backs are no longer to me.

Dagon puts an arm on the bartender's shoulder. "I hear you, man."

Dagon's smile is wicked.

Evil.

"When you came to me the first time, Jeffery, you had such promise. You were a rising star in the country world. You thought money would secure your prospects. You wanted to rub shoulders with the folks who made the deals," Dagon says.

Jeffery nods. "I did. I do. I mean, yes," he takes a breath. "I learned the hard way; money isn't everything I thought it was."

"It's sad, really. No matter how often I warn folks that money won't buy them love or respect, they still believe they know better," Dagon shrugs and pats the bartender on the shoulder again, then impales him in the chest with his bare fingertips. Dagon's full hand sits inside Jeffery's chest cavity.

I wait for the light to leave his eyes, but it only happens after Dagon rips the man's heart out.

The bartender drops to the gravel drive. Dagon turns to me, beating heart in hand. "I've got your sacrifice. We can go now."

"I didn't ask for this," I say, unspilled tears blurring my vision. "I didn't ask for any of this."

"This, Scarlet, is exactly what you've asked for."

CHAPTER 15

DAGON

Scarlet asked for honesty.

I gave her honesty.

You showed her the monster.

I showed her honesty.

You wouldn't know honesty if it slapped you in the face.

Leave now while you can still die peacefully and on your own terms. In three moons, it will be an agonizing way to go.

I squash the voice of the ghost that lingers in this body.

"This, Scarlet, is exactly what you've asked for," I say, knowing she's not ready to trust me yet, regardless of how honest I am with her. "It's a dirty business making deals with human folk."

We walk in silence for a time before Scarlet breaks it. "How does someone strike a deal with a—" her voice cracks, "—demon?" Scarlet shrugs. "Hypothetically speaking."

"Are you looking for glory or fame?" I mock. "Or perhaps to be invisible?"

If Scarlet could fade into the background, I know she would. She never wants fame or glory. She's only ever dreamt of a quiet life.

In every reincarnation, she longs for the quiet of the country or an island.

"Ha. None of the above." She clears her throat. "I was just curious about the semantics."

Sure you are. Whatever you need to tell yourself, darling.

"It starts with a summoning spell. Not every Dick and Jane of the Darkness can boast a contract with humans. Those who can, require a trade," I let my words settle a moment before continuing. "A clever person would offer more than their soul. They'd do their research and know exactly who they're summoning and what it is that said demon or deity desires."

"What did he want?" Scarlet nods to the heart I carry in my right hand.

"Jeffery here wanted money. Like most of the poor shlubs. He traded his heart ten years ago to win the lottery."

"He won the lottery and was still in that dump?"

"It's not my business what they do with the money. But it's quite common to find someone in a worse place than where they started."

"You can just snap your fingers and make someone win the lottery?" she asks, eyes wide and alarmed.

"There is always a cost, Scarlet. The universe requires balance," I explain.

69

"Balance," Scarlet repeats.

"For every action, there is a counteraction."

"Are you saying nothing good happens without the price of something bad?"

"No. That's not what I'm saying at all. It's far more nuanced than that," I say, trying not to be annoyed. She's curious. That's a good thing. "Balance has to do with good and evil. It's not black and white. Magic has a cost."

"Can you make money out of thin air?" she asks.

I snap my fingers together and produce a one-hundred-dollar bill.

"That has a cost?" Scarlet asks.

"No. It's just paper."

Scarlet's brow furrows. "I don't understand."

I sigh, knowing full well that the intricacies of the cost of magic are beyond her grasp today. "Perhaps in time."

"Why his heart?" Scarlet asks, puzzled.

"Because he's a believer in the fiery pits of hell and doesn't want to land there after his death by trading his soul instead. So, he's trying to escape what is honestly a bit inevitable on his part—a wretched afterlife."

Fool.

Scarlet stops walking. "Is there a Hell?"

"Only for the true believers in such a monstrosity," I say.

"You're not a believer?"

"No."

"But you're a demon," Scarlet says, her tone flat.

I gesture at myself, "This wasn't my decision."

"Then whose?"

I let her question hang in the air.

"I want to tell you all of it. I will tell you all about it. But not until this spell is cast. I don't want you to doubt my words or intentions," I say.

Scarlet's shoulders slump. "Okay. What's next?"

"We just need a bit of dragon."

CHAPTER 16

SCARLET

"Dragon? As in once upon a time in a fairyland?" I say.

If he thinks I'm gullible, he's got another thing coming.

"Let me see if I have this correct," Dagon ticks points on his fingers. "Demons are real. Magic and portal transportation are real. You're the Fountain of Youth personified, but dragons are where you suspend belief in the supernatural?"

"I—I mean," I gulp. I've lost my words.

I hate him.

I cross my arms. "Where are we going to find a dragon?"

"Smaller ones are a bit easier to spot than the big ones. I'm not sure how much you'll see on your own," Dagon says.

"Why's that?"

"Because of your witchy friends." Dagon holds my eyes for a moment before releasing me. "The Circle has been around for hundreds of years. They've 'protected humans' at the cost of their sight," loathing drips from his lips. "Whatever they need to tell themselves to ease their guilty conscience."

The Circle can't.

They wouldn't.

"I don't understand," I say.

"Why should you?"

"CHICKENS?"

"Dragons."

"They're chickens," I say in disbelief.

We're on private farmland, in the middle of only the stars know where. The ocean is in the distance, and the faint sound of waves can be heard lapping against the cliffside.

"I warned you," Dagon says. "We only need a few feathers."

"Dragons have feathers?"

"Until recently, your kind believed that dinosaurs were featherless too," Dagon says.

I really don't understand.

If it looks like a chicken, clucks like a chicken, pecks like a chicken, chances are, it's a chicken.

As if he's reading my mind, Dagon says, "It's a dragon."

"I want to believe you, but—"

"I want you to believe me too. I want you to understand." Dagon blows out a breath and sits in the grass. He pats the ground next to him.

"Can you put that somewhere?" I ask.

Dagon holds up the heart. "You want to put it in your bag?"

"No," I say flatly. It's not going anywhere near my stuff.

"Then no."

I sit reluctantly.

Dagon reaches for my hand.

I pull away.

"Let me show you," he says.

Bile rises in my throat, twisting and knotting my stomach.

Deep breath, Scarlet.

A slow, deep breath.

I reach and take his hand.

Dagon's touch is fire on my skin.

"Ba, ru gu'e dam igi ki éšša ul, libir gibil gi-na," Dagon's deep whispered words are a secret to the universe.

Like a shield lifting, the jaws of oblivion release me. Before my eyes, the chicken shimmers and takes the form of a dragon.

I have no words.

The dragon is no bigger than a chicken. He has little horns that form a crown. Orange and iridescent blue feathers, talons, and all. There's a purplish fog surrounding this little beasty.

"What's in the air?" I ask. "Is it safe to breathe?"

"It's a type of gas the little ones produce. It's only dangerous in large quantities, but this amount is quite harmless."

"Little ones?"

"There are larger ones, too," he says.

"Do the larger ones also produce a noxious gas?" I ask.

"No. The larger ones produce fire. These are akin to domesticated dogs, descendants from wolves. They've been bred to be small and free from flames," Dagon says.

I observe the little thing for some time, circling the patch of grass near us. It cocks its head to one side, seemingly watching me.

"How smart are they?" I ask.

"Incredibly," Dagon says.

"Would it be okay if I pet it?" I ask.

"At the risk of your fingers, by all means," he says.

I weigh his words and decide that I will probably never get another chance.

Deep breath, Scarlet.

Slowly, I reach my hand out.

Dagon clears his throat. "Don't come at it from above. It's far more likely to attack and bite you. Lower your palm and move slowly from the ground. It's considered less threatening."

I try not to roll my eyes. I know he's only attempting to be helpful. Even if I'd rather lose a finger than accept his help.

After another deep breath, I lower my hand to the ground instead of approaching the dragon from above.

It follows me with one eye, like a bird. I note its sharp talons and find the courage to keep my hand there longer.

Slowly, I raise my hand and stroke its feathers.

The little dude makes a deep throaty noise, *grack*.

I don't know if that's a good sign or not, but I give him another stroke.

He ruffles his feathers, blinking at me. *Grack.*

"Can I have him?" I ask before I realize what I've said.

Dagon raises a brow. "I don't think you understand what kind of undertaking he would be."

"It's a boy?" A warmth fills my chest. "I'll call him Augustus."

"When I let go of your hand, you will no longer be able to see him. Augustus will always appear to those under the veil of The Circle as a chicken," Dagon says.

"And I'm under the veil," I say, putting the puzzle pieces together.

"For now," Dagon says.

This grabs my attention, but I don't press the issue.

For now?

For now.

A shiver runs down my back. I stroke Augustus once more.

It's probably for the best, little dude. I don't know how to care for a dragon. Nor do I have a home for one. I can just imagine the looks I'd get from folks carrying a chicken everywhere.

And yet, I'm struggling to see how having Augustus in my life would be a bad thing.

Damn, Dagon.

"Who lives here? Do they know they're harboring a dragon?"

Dagon actually laughs at me.

He laughs!

Ass.

"This land belongs to a selkie I know," Dagon says.

"Selkie. Like the seal?" I ask.

"They are so much more than that, Scarlet. But yes. She's a lovely woman who just fell in love. Love is a bugger. It will make you do crazy things, like give up the ocean just to be near the one who holds your heart," Dagon's voice takes on a far-off feel. As if he's speaking from experience.

"Did you make a deal with her?"

"Yes."

"Will you be taking her life, too?"

"In a sense, I already have," he says. "She traded me her skin. I may use it and do what I see fit for as long as she is human."

"And when she's done being human?"

"Then she will return to the sea, never to touch land again," Dagon says somberly. He pockets two feathers plucked directly off the dragon. "I've got what we came for."

Chapter 17

Kara

It's been months since Zig and Scarlet ran off to, well, who knows where. Stars know what they were thinking.

Stupid children.

Careless.

Unthinkable.

Azeltha tried to explain that someone within The Circle had compromised our security. They compromised the safety of Scarlet.

Scarlet.

Stupid girl.

But that doesn't matter. This is no way to handle the situation.

We meet and vote as a unit.

The Circle's success depends on our rules and carefully thought-out procedures.

None of this side quest nonsense.

Who do they think they are?

Joe clears his throat, reminding me of his presence.

I reach for my tea, biding my time.

"We need to talk about replacing Zig," Joe says.

"No," I shake my head. "It's too soon."

"They're gone. We have to face reality. Zig or Scarlet could be possessed right now, and we'd be none the wiser. If they were coming back, they would have done so," Joe, the King of Coney—as he likes to call himself—won't meet my eyes.

Hurt and anger roll off him, carving holes of pain and anxiety through the psychic shield I keep up. I can't tell if it's aimed at me for not doing more or just part of him right now.

"I'm sorry, Joe. I know better than most what Zig means to you. We will find him. I'll beat him senseless, but we'll find him first," I say with as much empathy as I can offer. "I promise, if it's the last thing I do, I will personally find Zig."

Joe nods slowly. "I'm not ready to say goodbye either. But we must consider the bigger picture. If we lose the human wards, we lose everything. It will be the Salem witch trials all over again. Only this time, there are weapons of mass destruction involved."

"You know they never killed any actual witches, Joe. Stop perpetuating rumors that it was anything but fear-mongering by controlling assholes who would rather judge than act with kindness. All because of power."

"And yet you knew exactly what I meant," Joe says. "Zig is dangerous. If anyone knew what he was actually capable of... Our only saving grace might be that Zig doesn't know."

I can't let my mind go to the worst-case scenario.

Not yet.

"Perhaps Justine could shadow you for a while. Just until Zig is back," I say. "He will be back so you can teach him all he has yet to learn."

"Send her in my place to the next meeting. She can get her feet wet," Joe says.

"You could always show up yourself, you know," I say.

"I hate them. The only reason I'm on the damn council is out of my control. Don't bother arguing with me. You know I'm right."

"I know that I respect you and value your opinions, which has nothing to do with an ability you were born with. You could be a right ass, and I wouldn't be enjoying this tea with you."

Joe smiles, and we sip our tea in silence.

CHAPTER 18

SCARLET

Dagon draws symbols into the earth. The first looks like four spirals turning in on themselves. The second symbol he draws is the Dara Knot. I know this symbol from my studies to mean truth and wisdom.

He chants as he carves the earth. In the center of a circle, Dagon places the turtle scrapings, the dragon's feathers, and the human heart.

"Place the daffodils in the circle, Scarlet," Dagon says.

I place them gently, careful to avoid the blood.

Dagon pulls a key from his pocket and places it with the flowers. Then, he removes his ring and adds it to the growing pile.

He removed Zig's ring.

My ring.

"Universe, wisdom, love, respect, bravery, honesty, humility, and truth," Dagon says. In one hand, he holds a knife. The other is stained with the life of another.

Dagon finds my eyes and lifts the knife.

Stupid.

Stupid.

Stupid.

What am I doing?

Dagon slices his wrist open with the blade.

He sliced Zig's wrist.

Fuck.

Dagon holds the knife out to me.

Hesitantly, I take it.

Dagon nods to me, holding his hand out to my own.

I lift my wrist to the sky and slice.

Dagon takes a step toward the sacrificial circle, and I match his movements. He drips life force onto the earth and to the gods above.

I do the same.

Dagon straightens, and when he speaks, words slip off his tongue into the last light of the day. "Universum, sapientia, amor, reverentia, virtus, honestas, humilitas, veritas. Sacrificium sanguinis. Sacrificium amoris. Tenetur honestus in verbis et in corde. Cohaeret sanguine et veritate."

He looks to me, but I don't dare speak.

Slowly, Dagon says, "Universum, sapientia, amor."

"Universum, sapientia, amor," I repeat. We continue a slow back and forth until I've repeated the entirety of the unknown spell.

The blood spell.

As the sun is eclipsed by the earth until another dawn, a glow encircles us. Warmth spreads through my body. A cord of truth connects me to Dagon.

Only when the last light has left us does Dagon speak. "It's done."

"No more lies?"

"None."

"How will I know for sure?" I ask.

Dagon raises a brow, and a wicked smile teases at his lips. "My name is Stanford, and I am a unicorn."

There's a pull inside me. It's uncomfortable but not painful in any way.

"I loathe thee, Scarlet," his words somehow a sudden snarl.

The cord pulls uncomfortably tighter and catches in my chest.

"I am Dagon."

I feel nothing.

No sharp pull, no uncomfortable tug. No tightness in my chest.

Nothing.

"Settled?" Dagon asks.

"For now."

CHAPTER 19

MARCUS

I f there is one thing I've learned as a telepath in the magical community, it's that everything has an origin, and demons taste like maggots.

Truth has a source.

Death is a foul flavor. It doesn't go away no matter how much I try to wash it out of my mouth, eat something, or even brush my teeth.

Death tastes the worst.

There's a lot about mermaids I couldn't begin to comprehend a few days ago. I always assumed they were something Disney made up. Truthfully, they got their mermaid story from Hans Christian Andersen. But the thing is, they are way older than even that. Way older than I could have ever imagined. And their origin is spread across the entirety of Earth.

It's kind of incredible.

If it wasn't also so terrifying.

There are stone carvings in Ancient Assyria of a goddess named Atargatis with a woman's upper body and a fish's lower body.

Mermaid!

Ancient Greece is chock-full of references to mermaids. They called them sirens. Apparently, they lured sailors to their deaths with their enchanting voices. Because it's not enough for the mermaids to be deities or princesses; they can also just sing you to death.

Fucking mermaids of death?

I'm starting to think that mermaids are not only legit but that there's more to this world than I understand.

Of all people, I feel like I should be on the list of folks who understand. How can they train me as a council member for The Circle and leave me in the dark?

The goddess Isis, in Egyptian mythology, was depicted with mermaid qualities. They called her the goddess of the sea. Ancient India, Scandinavia, Rome, Scotland, Russia, Brazil, Japan, Melanesia, Arabia, Ireland, the Philippines, Maori, Finland, Africa, Persia, the Inuit, and Indigenous cultures ALL have depictions of mermaids.

And that's just grazing the surface.

And here, I thought it was limited to Disney movies and Australian television shows.

Sometimes, mermaids are supposed to be the spirits of the drowned. Other times, they're gods or goddesses of the ocean, land, or entire towns.

They are almost always the most stunning creatures in the known land.

Except when they're terrifying, like the Iara, the Nøkken, the ii-merdiwa, the nykr, the abere, or the magindara.

Sometimes, mermaids are part seals. Other times, they're part deer or bird.

But they're always part fish.

Mermaids have an origin.

Dagon has an origin, too.

The only thing I'm confident of is that my understanding of this world will continue to shift with every question I ask.

Even still, it's pretty lame.

Dagon being a mermaid makes me chuckle to myself.

Or he was a mermaid, as in past tense? I don't understand how that could be. I wonder briefly if he still is or has the ability. Like once a mermaid, always a mermaid? Or are demon mermaids a thing? Did he lose his mermaid abilities when he became a demon?

Azeltha said not to take mermaids lightly.

I move through my stacks of papers again, absorbing everything I can.

Abuela doesn't allow internet at Mundi. She claims magic moves through the same wavelengths that the Wi-Fi does. I don't even think she knows what Wi-Fi is, but she slapped the back of my head when I said as much.

I suggested we give it a try anyway. However, Abuela lost it on me at the mere idea of having strangers in Mundi to even set it up. No matter that I could set it up without them. She dug her heels in and insisted it would disrupt the magic.

Ultimately, Abuela is convinced that our library and rare

book collection is beyond anything she can find online. My Abuela, smarter than the internet.

I'm still rolling my eyes at her.

My books and loose stacks are organized into piles based on each bit of lore's potential darkness.

"You're going about this all wrong," Azeltha says suddenly.

I nearly pee myself. "Please stop doing that."

"You're not going to find what you're looking for in these books. History is told by the winners, Marcus." Azeltha sits across from me and rifles through one of my stacks.

"Why can't you just use the door like a normal person?" I ask.

"It's not about good and evil," she says, flipping pages.

"Or try announcing yourself before you just sneak up on me?"

"Do you think that Dagon was always the darkness?" Azeltha asks.

"If it smells like a maggot and tastes like a maggot, I'm going to go out on a limb and say it's a maggot." I close the books on the desk, stacking them neatly to one side.

"Nothing and no one is created evil," Azeltha says.

"How can you say that? How can you stand here with everything that has happened and defend it?"

"Until you're willing to understand all parts of someone, Marcus, you'll never see them for who they are and what they are capable of."

"It is a murderer," I spit my words.

"If you don't understand someone's motivations, they

will keep eluding your efforts to capture, rescue, or kill," Azeltha says.

"Why didn't you just say that?"

I hate when she plays the teach-Marcus-a-lesson game.

So annoying.

"I might seem annoying to you, boy, but you know I'm right. So, ditch the ego. Unless you've forgotten your commitment so quickly?" Azeltha looks me up and down coldly.

"Of all the people in my life, how could you say that?"

"Of all the people in your life, I'm the only one who can." Azeltha's words hang heavy as I think about the decisions she's made.

Her ego got in the way, and Kelby died as a result.

Scarlet died.

My Scarlet.

Just as quickly as she appears in the library, Azeltha disappears, leaving me to my thoughts.

CHAPTER 20

DEAR JENSEN

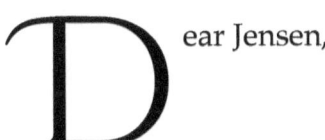ear Jensen,

IT'S BEEN TWO DAYS SINCE I MADE A BLOOD OATH WITH THE
Darkness.

With Dagon.

I didn't know he could use magic.

But he did.

We did.

There's a connection between us now.

At first, I thought this was what I wanted. I needed to
know every time Dagon lied to me. I couldn't fathom a
continuous walk through the dark without a light.

I would survive by any means necessary. This was a sacrifice I was willing to make.

But in actuality, I'm afraid I know all of Dagon's feelings.

I can't exactly ask him to be sure.

What if it was a mistake?

He thought he was doing a truth spell, and it turns out he was doing a telepathy spell instead, just to mess with me.

Or maybe it is a truth spell, but neither of us knew that knowing more than the other intended was part of the connection that bonds us.

Can he read my emotions too?

Or is it one way?

It's not exactly something I can confide in anyone else about.

Not that there is anyone.

Zig is gone.

I can't reach Marcus.

Kara is no different than Azeltha or the rest of the council. They'd all see me dead if they knew a fraction of what's passed between Dagon and me.

Zig too.

Perhaps not Azeltha. I'm not always sure which team she's playing for. It might just be that she's only playing on her own.

Dagon made some lofty promises. No matter what he says, trusting a demon feels wrong.

Probably because it is wrong.

So, fucking wrong.

I know this, and yet here I am. Trusting the damn demon.

I'm trying to trust myself, but I don't know how.

Doubting everything I knew to be true a little more with each passing day.

Doubting truths.

Doubting history.

Doubting memories.

One day at a time is all I can promise.

That might not be enough.

SCARLET

Chapter 21

Scarlet

"Would you tell me where we're going?" I ask for the second time. Dagon ignores me. I hate being ignored just about as much as I hate being here. He strides across the street effortlessly. Shoulders set back, tall, as if everything else is gum on the sidewalk.

Down the rabbit hole, I go. Where it leads, nobody knows.

Dagon stops and holds his hand out for mine.

"You going to share with the class where you think you're taking me?" I cross my arms.

"You agreed to follow me," Dagon says flatly.

"After you remove yourself from my friend," I remind.

"If I could snap my fingers and leave, I would," he growls.

"This is the thing I haven't been able to understand," I say. "It's been itching the back of my mind for days now. You can leave anytime you want, so why the delay?"

"You'd rather I pick some random person off the street and take their body instead? Is that better? Is that what you want, Scarlet?"

There's a tug at the thread that ties us. It's uncomfortable.

"What aren't you saying?"

"We have to summon an old acquaintance of mine. That's where we're going."

It's an easy truth to hide whatever is making him uncomfortable. Whatever he's lying about.

"More demons?" I ask.

"Why do you always go to the worst-case scenario, Scarlet?"

"Oh, I don't know, let me think," I rub my chin. "There was that time when my dad died. Oh, how about when a demon murdered my mom? Being hunted for the last several years, non-stop. Losing my friends, my life. Let's see, there was that—"

"I get it, okay. I didn't do those things."

The invisible rope grows tight around my insides. "Stop lying to me."

"Omission isn't a lie."

"It's called the lie of omission for a reason." I might not know the whole story, but I know he's behind it somehow. Mom is gone because of him.

Dagon's eyes narrow. He exhales and puts his hands up. "I didn't kill your mom."

The rope, which is wrapped tightly around my insides, loosens, and I feel nothing.

"I never told that putrid underling to kill her."

More truths.

"What about the sigil he drew in my Aech's blood? My poor cat. What about the fact that it was you he was summoning to our home?" I'm practically spitting my words. "You can't stand here and pretend like you're innocent."

"I won't pretend I'm innocent of anything. I'm ancient, Scarlet. I've done many things I'm not proud of."

Another evasion.

"Is there anything I can say that would earn your trust?"

"No."

We've been to a dozen markets in Karachi, and I'm still not sure what we're looking for. Dagon says he'll know it when he sees it. Which is absolute crap. He could tell me what he's looking for, try a bit of that honesty and communication he killed a man for. Instead, he ignores my questions.

Irritation burrows deeper into my skin.

Dagon moves his fingers slowly across intricate glass bottles of every color. Some are large enough to be considered a jug, while others are small enough for a few drops of perfume. I'm afraid to bump something in here and watch it all come crashing down around us. Shockingly, I don't drop or knock over a single glass object.

We visit a shop that has necklaces reminiscent of my own. I hold mine close to my chest, remembering the strength it provides me. This necklace was magically passed down from my lives lived before. The memories locked away are still a wonder to me. I know I've only relived a fraction of what it holds. In time, if I survive this, I want to learn more. I want to understand where I came from. Why I'm here. Who I was.

"Anything?" I venture.

"I'm looking for a particular kind of trinket," Dagon says.

"Yeah, I've gathered as much. And if you told me more, I might actually be able to help move this process along," I try not to roll my eyes but fail.

"Are you a historian?" he asks.

"No."

"Are you able to recognize the life pulse of ancient artifacts?"

"No."

"Can you remember what relics from your previous reincarnations look like?"

"Fine. I'll just stand here and look pretty."

"Good, you are excellent at that," Dagon says.

My cheeks flush at his compliment. Then I cringe. "Don't say things like that."

"I only speak truths now, remember?" Dagon never stops admiring necklaces throughout our conversation. He fingers a few more, and I watch him, annoyed.

"When you find what you're looking for, let me know," I say, ready to ditch.

"Found it," he says.

"Well, that was quick," I say, examining his choice.

"I told you I'd know it when I saw it. Trust, dearest, trust."

"I'm not your dearest," I say.

The necklace has simple beadwork alternating between a blue stone and a clear stone. At the bottom hangs a gold coin engraved with a sun. I don't know much about jewelry, but it looks time-worn, and there's a slight vibration to it. As if touching it might shock me somehow.

"For your lady?" the shopkeeper asks.

"Yes, thank you," Dagon smiles.

"A lovely choice. This pair of earrings," from seemingly nowhere, the clerk pulls out a pair of matching jewels, "would go perfectly."

"That's okay," I say. "I'm not his lady."

"Ahh," the clerk removes the earrings and offers the box with the necklace tucked safely away.

"Cheeky," Dagon leers.

"Since you're buying, I'll take that knife," I point to a delicate golden dagger.

"What are you going to do with that?" Dagon raises a brow.

"Can't I just have something because it's beautiful?"

"Not hardly."

"It's just a little something to remember this trip by."

"We'll take the knife as well," Dagon says.

I smile to myself.

He and I both know I don't need a blade to protect anything or anyone. No weapon can do what my hands are capable of. I just wanted to know if he'd buy it because I asked.

He did.

CHAPTER 22

DAGON

I don't like little human games. I don't partake in their ridiculous rituals. Humans are infantile, and I refuse to bow to their petty diversions. Fear of death is their only motivator. I fear nothing.

"Where are we now?" Scarlet asks.

"The Dead Sea, in Jordan," I say.

"I—" Scarlet quiets, taking in the view. Her mouth is open slightly in awe.

I can acknowledge its beauty. There are still some places that manage to steal my breath. Some people, too.

"Why is it called the Dead Sea?" Scarlet asks.

"There's too much salt in the water. No plant life or sea life can survive," I say.

"Oh."

"Come, I'm hoping an old friend is still here."

"A friend?" Scarlet's words are a question, as if I can't have friends.

To be fair, I don't really have many friends. Or any.

"I can't imagine she'll be too excited to see me. But considering not many folks know she's here, perhaps this one time, she'll reconsider her inevitable rage," I say.

"Should I be worried?" Scarlet runs her fingers through her hair absentmindedly.

"You are in a mortal body. I assume you should always worry," I say.

She huffs but follows in silence.

There's time to enjoy the sandy banks, so I plop down and remove my shoes, letting my feet warm in the sand. I close my eyes and let the last of the sun kiss my skin.

Scarlet clears her throat.

"Try enjoying the moment," I say without opening my eyes.

"You're just going to sunbathe?" Scarlet asks.

"Yep."

"And I'm supposed to what?"

"Soak in the weather, dip your toes in the water, or just enjoy the view."

Scarlet sighs.

When I feel the sun lower behind the horizon, I slip my shoes back on, stand up, and stretch.

There are rules in the human world, and there are rules in the supernatural world. Most of them do not overlap. Every once in a while, however, they do. I pull the talisman out of my pocket.

Never visit an old friend empty-handed. Always remember a gift, especially when you're an unwelcome guest. Lastly, never go into a situation with an old foe without providing yourself an out.

Scarlet stands back, watching from what she believes is a safe distance.

Safe is irrelevant when dealing with a Marid.

CHAPTER 23

SCARLET

Dagon tosses the necklace into the water. I go to stop him but quickly remember I have zero idea why I'm bothering. I step back instead.

We wait. It's a solid fifteen minutes before anything happens. In fact, I'm about ready to suggest leaving and trying elsewhere for this elusive "friend" when she suddenly appears. The sea begins to gurgle and burp. The once-calm water seems to effervesce.

But how?

As if tiny waves were bubbling from the middle of the sea, a storm without wind, something—or someone—was rising from the water. I stumble backward, trying to put more space between myself and whatever this being is.

As the creature ascends, I note her iridescent hair, gray eyes, and gray-blue skin. She is tall. Captivating. It's like she is part of the water. She is inescapably beautiful.

"Did you think you could just leave me here and call me again at your will?" she says, her torso rising out of the water. "Did you think I would forget who you are if you changed your face?"

She doesn't have legs. It's more like she's one with the water. A shadow comes over her as she speaks, and the sea rises around her. She wears it like clothing. I take another step backward. She is terrifying. As if by her sheer will alone, I could suddenly drown on dry land.

"Hello, Nameera," Dagon says to the water woman.

"How dare you show yourself," Nameera says. In her hand is the necklace Dagon offered the Dead Sea.

"After all this time, I thought you'd be excited to see me," Dagon says.

There's a tug at my insides. He's lying to her.

"I'd rather spend eternity here than waste any more life on you," Nameera says.

"Really? I thought you'd be bored after a few days in the Dead Sea," Dagon looks to the stars. "I can't imagine how you've survived the last three hundred years. It must be so dull. Nothing endures in the Dead Sea. Well, nothing except you."

Nameera moves the necklace from one hand to the other, admiring it. "What do you want, Dagon?"

"You owe me," Dagon says.

"I owe you nothing," Nameera is forceful. The water grows choppier, and she becomes a bit taller. "She lives. That was the deal."

"You thought you could pull one over on me?"

Nameera's eyes narrow. "Is she breathing?"

Dagon growls, "Yes."

"Does her heart pump blood?"

"Do not belittle me."

"And yet here I am," Nameera stretches her arms out and circles in the sea, rising higher and higher, the water rising with her. "You came here to mock me, Dagon," her voice is deeper. "Why should I let you walk away twice?"

"I will grant you a favor," Dagon says, standing his ground.

"I need nothing from you."

"Don't kid yourself, Nameera. You've been stuck here, alone, for three hundred years. I would apologize for leaving you here, but I am not repentant." Dagon stands taller. "I need something from you, and you need something from me. This is just a little mutually beneficial help."

"I can't change what's been done," the fountain of water beneath Nameera shrinks slightly.

"I understand," Dagon sighs. "I need a body."

"What's wrong with the one you've stolen?" she asks.

Dagon's jaw tightens. There's a slight tug at my chest. He doesn't want to be honest with her.

"I want my body back," he says.

"Your body is long ago decayed, now one with the earth," Nameera measures him with her eyes.

"That has never stopped you before," Dagon says.

"True." Nameera's fountain lowers until she is at eye level again. "Beneath Caribbean waves, a treasure concealed. A lamp of magic, by water's grace, revealed. Emerald depths unveil my watery lair; I am the Marid of oceans with ethereal flair. Grasp the lamp, its glow in hand. A wish fulfilled by sea and its strand. In this sacred space, Caribbean's secrets are a goddess's home, found only in the ocean's embrace."

Without another word, Nameera is gone. Only when the water returns to its original calm, without a ripple in sight, do I tread lightly forward and find my voice. "What does that mean?" I ask.

"That means we have our work cut out for us," Dagon runs a hand through his hair.

"We have to solve a riddle, and then you get a wish?" I ask.

"We have to solve a riddle, find something for her, and then we get a wish," Dagon says.

"A body for you?" I ask, hoping this means there's still hope for Zig.

Dagon nods solemnly. "If we can find what she asks for, then yes. A body for me."

PART TWO

BEGINNINGS

*"There will come a time when you believe everything is finished;
that will be the beginning."*

Louis L'Amour

CHAPTER 24

AZELTHA

Scarlet and Dagon stand on the edge of the water's bank. There is no fight between them. When the Dead Sea rises to meet Dagon in the form of a woman, I expect Scarlet to use the opportunity to run.

Only she doesn't.

She stays with the demon.

Maybe she's still in the dark. Maybe she doesn't know it's not Zig.

After all, I didn't know Zig was gone for a long time, either. I cannot be sure if she is being deceived by him or not.

I could get her alone.

If she knew that Zig was really—I can't finish the thought.

It's too horrific for even me.

Oh, Zig. Mi nieto.

I watch the three of them for a long time. The woman of the sea is likely a type of Djinn. A Marid, if I'm not mistaken.

These may be old eyes, but they still work well. How she found herself so far from the open ocean is a brain tickler.

It would be too dangerous to get any closer or let myself be seen. Dagon can't be trusted, and I'm not strong enough to take him down alone. As a result, I can't hear the words exchanged between the three.

When the woman sinks back to the sea and the water goes still, I depart.

Zig is no more.

Dearest Kelby, I can't help you if you won't help yourself.

CHAPTER 25

SAUVIGNON

JOURNAL ENTRY

It does not matter where I go. Where I hide. They always find me. Eventually, the Darkness will find me too.

My sentinel is gone. She's been gone for so many weeks I've lost track of the days. Maybe it's months now. I have forgotten how to count the days. I tried to track them in my head, and when that became too hard, I tried to mark the days on the floor and the walls of this cell. Eventually, I lost the ability to do that, too. They magicked away my markings and called them dirty.

They called me dirty. I'm not dirty. This was supposed to be a safe place. My sentinel trusted these people. They were her people. They were supposed to protect me from the others. Until they found out I was an other.

That's why they called me dirty. When they thought I was human, they were ready to go to the ends of the earth to save me. The moment I wasn't normal, I was something they used to their own ends. They slit my wrists whenever someone needed blood from me.

Life tied to a chair. Locked in a cell. Less than human. My blood lengthens lives and heals the injured. It exorcises demons while creating more of my own every time I close my eyes. Exploited for the very gift I am supposed to save this world with. I mean nothing to these people except for what I can provide them.

I never did. The Circle is no better than the demons. They might be worse. At least the demons do not hide behind what they are. The Circle pretends to be the righteous champions for humanity.

Monsters. The whole piss of them. Let the Darkness come. Let him take me in. I invite him to this cage. We will destroy The Circle first. Then, we will destroy one another. And finally, death will be mine.

Death will be a sweet release after months in this witch-built purgatory. Every minute in this place is an eternity I want to forget. Cleanse my mind of their evil and set me free from every soul who said they would protect me, who only betrayed me instead. And from every person who claimed to care who was easily swayed by the promise of everlasting health over treating me as a human or former friend.

No one asked. No one sought my consent. The worst part is that I would have helped them if they had only asked. Instead, they took. And took. And took. They stole my life. My blood. My soul. Tied me up as if my life was worth less somehow.

There is nothing left worth living for. Nothing left worth fighting for. I will bargain with the Darkness. It can have anything. There is nothing it could offer that would be worse than what I've survived. I would give myself over just to escape.

The day comes when my sentinel breaks in. At first, I thought she was a ghost. She spoke my name with such a softness. My sentinel was all but a shadow on the wall. She spoke a spell into my ear from a distance. Her magic was always strong. She nodded at me, urging me on. I repeated the words aloud. They wrap around me slowly, moving through my parts, burning a path to my center.

They are the last words this body ever speaks. I don't fight the end. I embrace it. I close my eyes, and I am gone.

CHAPTER 26

SCARLET

A body for Dagon.

Saving Zig.

It's almost too much to wrap my head around. I don't know how long it will take Dagon to puzzle out the riddle. I only remember a little of it, and he doesn't need or want my help.

As if I, a puny human, could help him.

We leave Jordan through a portal in the middle of a bridge and step out the other side into the blistering, sticky heat.

"Where are we?" I ask, already pulling at my top for some air.

"We are on one of the Caribbean islands," Dagon says.

"That doesn't narrow it down much. Aren't there more than a dozen countries in the Caribbean?" I think back to geography class. Unfortunately, I don't remember much more than that.

"Why does it matter?"

"Transparency matters. I thought we'd established that already. My mistake," I say, baiting him.

He doesn't bite.

We don't walk far before reaching a dirt road. There's a black car waiting for us. I want to ask how someone knew we'd be here, but he'd probably ignore that question, too. Besides, I've never seen him use a cell phone, and I don't think I want to know how the Demon network works just yet.

The Caribbean is warmer than I expected. I mean, I knew it would be warm—but it's warm times humid, multiplied by the square root of hot.

The dirt road goes on for a long while. I stare out the window and take in the view.

Whatever island we're on, it's private.

In the distance is a large white building. "Are we here to nick something from the museum?" I ask. "Did you solve the riddle?"

Dagon clicks his tongue. "That is not a museum, Scarlet."

I glance out the window again, noting the lack of signage as we grow closer. It's slightly reminiscent of Pemberley from Pride and Prejudice.

I shake the ridiculous thought away.

"This is yours?" I ask.

"Ownership is all relative. But for the sake of your meaning, yes," Dagon says.

There's movement on the cord that binds us, but it's not tight or even closing in. It was an honest truth, but—I don't know?

Something feels off.

"How long are we here for?" I ask.

"This is our home, Scarlet. We will come and go from here, but we will always come back," Dagon glances at me, watching for a reaction.

"I don't have a home."

"You do now."

The driver pulls to a stop. When I step out of the car, I'm hit with the balmy heat all over again. Immediately, I start sweating.

"I promise you will acclimate," Dagon says, leading the way up twenty-two steps to the front door.

"I've never enjoyed sticky climates. I don't imagine I'll ever get used to this," I say. Not even if I get to live in a Jane Austen novel.

Not that demons, witches, dragons, and whatever else this crazy world is hiding are in an Austen novel.

But still.

"I promise air conditioning is a luxury we have. Martin will take your things and show you to your room," Dagon says.

"No one touches my things," I say.

Martin looks affronted.

"Sorry, no offense. I'm perfectly capable of carrying the one bag I own," I say, eyeing Dagon suspiciously.

"I'm not trying to pull one over on you. Martin is my butler. He will attend to whatever needs you have, or he will ask one of the other employees," Dagon says.

"You have servants?"

"Employees," he corrects.

"Right."

"This way, Miss," Martin says, leading me up the grand staircase and down a long hallway. He stops before a large double door and pulls a large skeleton key from his pocket. "This one is yours, Miss." Martin opens the door for me.

Of course, it locks from the outside. Why did I expect anything different?

I take a breath and step into the space.

Martin follows, opening the drapes to the floor-to-ceiling windows, letting light into the darkened room. "You'll find everything you need here. The restroom is over here," he says, opening another door. "There are fresh towels, soap, and toothbrushes there. Let me know if you need anything. The staff has been instructed to fulfill whatever shopping requests you have."

"Thank you," I say.

Martin turns to go.

"One more thing," I say before he's gone. "Can I have the key to this room, please?"

He turns, pulls the key from his pocket, and hands it to me. "Certainly."

I didn't expect that. "Uh, thanks."

"Will you need anything else, Miss?"

"No."

Martin leaves. I take a turn about the room, chuckling to myself.

This is ridiculous.

Insane, really.

The king-size canopy bed is calling my name. It might sound crazy, but maybe this is a chance to actually relax. Read a book and catch up on Earth's rotations after hiding in every dark corner for the last several months.

Maybe that's incredibly selfish.

No, it is.

But it's not like I have friends or family.

No comforts of home. I can only hope the food is good and the bed is soft.

Plus, I need time away from him.

Space to process the last few days.

Sleep.

Gods above, I need sleep. All the sleep I can get. I'm so tired. I don't know if it's the spells, the portaling, or the emotional stress. I just want to crawl into this bed and never crawl out again.

A landline phone sits on the desk, which faces one of the large windows on the far side of the room. On the adjacent wall is a large library of books.

My heart leaps out of my chest when realization hits.

The first number that comes to mind is my mother's. An ache the size of Seattle rips a fresh wound in my chest. I take a deep breath, remembering I can't call her. After she passed, Kara had all of Mom's accounts closed. So even if I could call her, there would be no voicemail to listen to.

The problem with technology is that it requires nothing extra from your brain concerning memory. Mom would talk about how, in the "old days," she would have to memorize phone numbers, but now we just plug them into our cell phones.

She was right.

I don't know Marcus's number. I don't know Kara's or anyone from The Circle. Even with a phone, I can't do anything.

Suddenly, I have an idea.

I reach for the phone and dial zero. I'll ask the operator, and they'll have to connect me, right?

A man answers, "Ms. Singer, is there something I can get you? Is your room to your satisfaction?" It's not Martin, but someone else.

"I'm hungry. Could someone bring me something to eat?" I say, not wanting it to get back to Dagon that I was trying to call an operator.

"Of course. Was there anything in particular you wanted?" he asks. "Chef can make just about anything you'd like, or we can send someone to town."

I think for a moment, "I'd love some sparkling water and pepperoni pizza."

"I'll have Martin bring it up when it's ready. Anything else, Ms. Singer?"

"Do you have chocolate donuts?" I say.

"Of course."

"That's all. Thank you," I say and hang up.

Well, there's a phone, but unless I know a phone number, it only connects to the rest of the house. Hell, for all I know, it doesn't dial outside numbers.

• • •

I'VE SEEN DAGON TWICE SINCE WE ARRIVED AT PEMBERLEY. YES, I've taken to calling this place Pemberley. While it's not as cold as Britain would be this time of year, it's still beautiful. I'm thankful for the air conditioning.

The first opportunity I had to wander on my own, I took it. The great hall was on the main floor, down the grand staircase. The black and white checkered floor was almost dizzying. Every step reinforced how alone I was.

When I looked up, I lost my breath. The ceiling was just how I always imagined it, with a hand-painted sky. It was always the most perfect night sky, no matter the time of day. A fireplace in the middle of the room is larger than my bed at Mundi. The extravagance of this place knows no end.

I made my way to the library and was swept away by the opulence. It made the library in my room feel infantile when, only a day before, it had been the grandest thing I'd seen in years.

There is an open doorway to a drawing room where a large, lavish, dark wooden desk sits in the middle. I doubled back to the library, not wanting to find myself on the wrong side of Dagon's misplaced wrath.

Back in the safety of the books, I run my fingers across the leather spines. Unlike the ones in my bedroom, these looked as if they truly belonged in Pemberley—leather of varying colors, gold-embossed pages. I take one and sit on a couch.

Maybe I could disappear here forever, blend into the background, and forget about the woes of this world.

. . .

EACH TIME I SAW DAGON, HE WAS CARRYING A NOTEBOOK. I caught a glimpse of part of the riddle Nameera spoke. I didn't read all his notes, but they were filled with theories and a plethora of pages.

I should help him.

I should want to help him.

But a small part of me revels in every single one of Dagon's failings. Then I think of Zig, and the guilt becomes overwhelming.

Zig, trapped.

A prisoner in his own body, and that reminder is the only thing that keeps me here.

A knock at the door pulls me out of my thoughts.

"Hello?"

"Miss Scarlet, I have a delivery for you."

I open the door, and Martin stands on the other side, holding out a golden tray. In the center is an envelope.

"Miss," he nods.

I take the letter and shut the door.

A small part of me considers tossing the letter right out the window, letting it be consumed by nature and eventually the sea.

But then I think of Zig and open it.

Dearest Scarlet,

I request your attendance for dinner this

evening at six pm. There's a small token of my gratitude under your bed.

    —D

I SET THE LETTER ON THE DESK, WALK OVER TO THE BED, AND hesitantly drop to my knees, revealing a large box.

Let it be a dead rabbit.

Please give me a reason to keep hating you vehemently.

My chest suddenly drowns in a sea of guilt. Here I am, enjoying the comforts of this beautiful home while Zig is trapped. Marcus—I don't even know what to say about Marcus. I can't let my thoughts continue.

They lead nowhere but to darkness.

I made a choice.

Now, I have to live with it.

Inside the box is a yellow sundress. It's light and airy, and I hate to admit how lovely it is. Underneath the dress is a book.

It's old. Timeworn. A journal, but more thoughtfully put together. I thumb through the pages. It's not a scattering of entries; instead, they seem methodical by name. Ishara, Heleena, and Beatrix are just a few. The names go on and on.

They're all written in the same loopy scrawl, which means they're not written by different women.

But who are they?

Why?

I flip to the first page, and there's a foreword.

Dearest Reader,

As I embark on this journey, I hope you will come with me. I will document everything as I remember it happening, with the hope that you will find a kinship in these pages. The mesmerist believes he can help me remember our past reincarnations.

I believe that the past will be the key to unlocking our future.

Always,
R

I CHECK THE CLOCK AND REALIZE I ONLY HAVE A FEW MINUTES until six. The need to know more is overwhelming. I slip on the dress and read the first entry about a woman named Sauvignon before I leave to meet Dagon.

On the other side of the door is Martin.

Surprise, surprise.

Martin escorts me to a candle-lit path. I nod goodbye and follow the flames to the beach, where a table and two chairs are waiting. Tall torches provide plenty of ambient light.

As I approach, Dagon steps from the shadows and pulls out a chair for me.

"Thank you," I say, sitting down.

"I thought we could use a chance to talk privately. I've also arranged dinner for the evening," Dagon says, taking his seat across from me.

I try not to cringe. I just want a—

"I ordered us pizza," Dagon says, completing my thought.

"I was just thinking about how good a pizza sounded," I say. "Not that all this exotic food isn't lovely. I just want something familiar."

A waiter arrives with two pizza boxes and bottles of water. He sets them on the table and leaves without a word.

"Is there a pizza joint nearby?" I ask.

"Demon, remember?"

"Right."

I open the first box and grab a slice. It's the best thing I've eaten in weeks. It's way better than the fancy thing the chef made the other day. I asked for pepperoni pizza, and he brought me bubbly bread with sliced meat and sauce. There was a severe lack of cheese, and I cried.

I cried over cheese.

Okay, it wasn't the cheese, but the cheese was the final straw.

I inhale the slice and go for a second. After the second slice, I set a third on my plate but take a minute to digest.

"What did Nameera do? You said she owed you," I ask, picking at my pizza, avoiding Dagon's eyes.

Dagon finishes the bite in his mouth and takes his time swigging down some water.

Unwilling to give him an out, I remain silent.

When he finally speaks, Dagon's voice is low and methodical. "Someday, you will understand how I brought your parts together."

"What's wrong with right now?" I ask.

"Did you get the book?" Dagon asks, sidestepping my question and avoiding my gaze.

"Yes."

"I promise I will answer all your questions. But I'd like it if you'd read the book first," he says.

There's no tug at my chest.

Somehow, I still don't know how to trust his words. "Who wrote it?"

"You did," Dagon says. "Well, you from many years ago."

No tug.

He speaks the truth.

"How?"

Dagon takes a deep breath. "The longer you connect with that medallion," he points to my necklace, "the more you will remember."

"That's how I understand it, at least," I say.

"It's not always good," Dagon says.

"I know."

"But sometimes it's not bad either."

I don't agree.

"Once in a while, you want to remember all of it, as in everything. The last time you sought out the past, you wrote it down in that book. You made me promise to leave it as is and to pass it to the next you who trusted me enough to believe its pages," Dagon adds another slice of pizza to his plate.

"What makes you think that I trust you?" I ask.

"I don't. But I think you understand how this blood bond works. If not in totality, at least enough to know when I'm lying," Dagon says, running a finger along the edge of his plate.

"So, what happens if I agree to read your book?"

"It was never my book, Scarlet. It was always waiting for you," Dagon says.

I pick at my pizza crust, refusing to meet his gaze.

"I'll answer all your questions. Anything you want to know. I will be the open book you request of me," Dagon says.

I finally meet his eyes. "Is Zig still in there?"

Dagon sits back in his chair and takes another swig of his water. His lip twitches. "Yes."

No tug.

"Okay. I'll read it."

Chapter 27

Zig

I'm here, Scarlet.

I'm not going anywhere.

Don't do anything stupid, Scar.

Don't trust him.

He has my face, but they're not my words.

CHAPTER 28

CLAIR

JOURNAL ENTRY

The seventh child, born on the seventh day of the seventh month, I was supposed to be a lucky omen —a gift from the gods above to bring prosperity and hope to my family.

Destined for greatness, I was educated not only in running a household but also in maths, business, and the local trades.

None of it came easily.

Maths was impossible for me to grasp. That didn't make understanding business any easier.

I am the youngest member of my family. Running a household requires respect, something I've never demanded and was never freely given.

"Speak up, Clair," my mum would say. "No one will listen to you if they can't hear you."

From an early age, I learned that you don't have to be

loud to be effective. There are other ways to accomplish your goals if one is creative enough.

The family would move so fast around me, never slowing down enough to see me.

I could do virtually anything, and no one would notice.

When I disappeared on the first day, I thought I would get the beating of a lifetime. But when I returned from my excursion, no one said anything.

Nothing.

Mum didn't even notice I'd been gone.

They never saw what I did in the shadows. There were folks who would listen to me. People who respected me, who saw and heard me.

I was a different person away from them.

When my parents' gifts were wasted on me—their words, not mine—I was married off to bring them the relief they worked so hard for.

One less mouth to feed. One less shame to bear in their home.

My family never knew about my real blessings.

They would have called it a curse. They would have never understood.

They did not know about the demons. How they walk among us as humans.

The Darkness wove its tendrils through me, and I breathed it in, letting it find threads to my core.

My family was relieved to see me go.

I was relieved, too.

I no longer had to hide who I was. I did not have to hide the death. I could hunt in peace without their prying eyes.

I could embrace who I really am.

All the ways that I was special. All the reasons I was the gift all along.

Don't fear the Darkness or what it holds in store for you, dear one. What we are capable of might surprise you.

Who we are.

Who we were always meant to be.

Chapter 29

Marcus

"There's no time to lose. We have to go now, Abuela," I say, practically jumping in my seat.

The council table at Max's has felt so cold in recent weeks. Privacy bubbles go up as soon as folks enter—if they come at all.

No one is here today. Only Abuela and I sit at the oversized, elaborate table. The high-back chairs sit empty, waiting in anticipation for their paired council members to pop into a meeting.

With the whole of The Circle on high alert, the representatives have had their hands full, squashing daily fears within their communities. Once word got out that one of the Voids was missing and that the Darkness might have taken him—well, let's just say it hasn't been pretty.

Trying to convince Abuela to listen to me for once in her

life instead of her own ego is no easy feat. I love her, but I'm so frustrated. I want to scream or shake her.

Just believe me!

Abuela is just staring at me.

"I don't know how long Gemma will stay in one spot. It's taken me months to find her. I'm not going to risk losing her again," I say. "After everything she's done, she needs to be brought here, to justice."

Abuela closes her eyes and sighs. "You can't go alone, mi Nieto. Take Joe with you."

"I'm not a child," I spit out in frustration. "I don't need a babysitter."

Abuela's eyes narrow. "Clearly, you do," she says, placing both hands on the table. I sit back in my chair. "Joe can protect you in ways that no one else can. After everything that's happened, we need him. You need him, Marcus. This is not up for debate."

"He couldn't even be bothered to show up today," I say, just as Joe pops into his chair. "Speak of the portaling devil."

"My ears were burning," Joe winks.

"Marcus believes he's got a lead on Gemma," Abuela explains.

"Zig?" Joe asks.

"She's our best lead," I say.

"Let's go." Joe stands.

I'm surprised at how quick his call to action is.

"Where are we going? What do I need to be prepared for? Fill me in because I don't like surprises," Joe says.

"Um, well, yes," I say, shaking away the surprise at the

unexpected support. "So, I was able to track her to an under-ground network of witches who stay off the grid. Like way off the grid. The connection goes back to a cousin of Gemma's. She's hiding in a flat. It's low profile, but nothing too out there. I have the address and am ready to go when-ever you are."

"Who's the cousin?" Joe asks.

"Someone by the name of Nikodemus. When I stumbled on the underground network, it was a bit hard to decipher at first. But eventually, I learned there were messages between Gemma and Nikodemus," I say. "I'm fairly confident they're related. What I'm not so confident about is how a subset of secret witches exists without The Circle's knowledge."

Abuela doesn't meet my eyes.

"So, not secret. Just not to my knowledge," I blow out a rage-filled breath. "I'm so sick of the lies."

"Alright, let's go," Joe says, standing. "Now."

"Fine," I say, following him.

"Be careful, Marcus," Abuela says.

"Yeah." I squeeze her shoulder on the way out. Despite my anger, she's still my Abuela.

When we reach the library, I pull the pen from the cup on Max's desk. On a scrap of paper, I write the letters CO. I reach for Max's universal portal.

"This should take us close to where Gemma is hiding," I say.

Joe grabs my shoulder, and I twist my ring with one hand while focusing on our location and holding the portal with the other.

Two seconds later, we arrive on the streets of Columbus, Ohio. "I've tracked Gemma to a building on Park Street downtown."

"Nicely done, Marcus," Joe claps me on the back. "Do you know why Kara asked me to come?"

"Because she has so little faith in me, she's convinced I need a babysitter," I say, a bit more peevishly than I intend.

"Because she knows I can do things that you can't even fathom," Joe smiles. "I've always enjoyed Columbus. Do you want to see a cool trick, Marcus?"

I shrug. "Sure."

Joe tilts his head and spins the simple gold band on his right ring finger. I watch as the world spins on its axis.

"What did you just do?" I hold onto the wall of a nearby building for balance. "I thought Voids couldn't do magic."

"Not strictly speaking. What I do is the opposite of magic," Joe says.

"I mean, I know. You're a Void, but—"

"But why is there a hot pink fog rolling around us?" Joe says with a Cheshire grin.

"And the woozy lack of magic in the air?"

"I've expanded my protection circle around you. By doing this, if Gemma casts a spell at you, it will stop at my void, acting as a circle of protection for both of us," Joe says.

"But I can't taste the magic anymore. It's like you've removed all the magic from the air. Is that possible? How? More importantly, why?"

"Well, that is the other side of the coin. I can remove her ability to use magic, but I'm also removing ours. I can't keep some of the magic." Joe shrugs. "It's an all-or-nothing kind of void."

"Why can't I smell or taste anything?" I ask.

"Your telepathy?"

I nod.

"It's not gone. It's just harder to notice. You'll need to focus and give it more of your attention until you are able to determine what your telepathy senses under these new conditions," Joe says.

"Man, why didn't Abuela just send a Void to school with me as a shield growing up? I might have had a chance at making it past elementary school," I say, half laughing, half horrified. The disjointed mix of emotions was the furthest thing from my thoughts when we landed and popped out of the portal.

I cast a tracker spell using one of Gemma's belongings. While not as good as blood, if we were within a two- or three-mile radius of Gemma, the tracking spell would take us to her. On the other hand, blood could track someone all over the globe.

"This way," I say, following the map I had tucked away in my back pocket.

The spell leads us to a third-floor walkup. We stand in front of a black door with gold trim.

"Are you ready for this?" Joe whispers.

"Nope. But I'll do whatever it takes to find Scarlet and bring Zig back alive," I say. My stomach does a flop, threatening to upheave breakfast.

"Good. I will drop the shield just long enough for you to

unlock the door. Then it goes right back up," Joe says, looking around, double-checking the space once more.

I nod.

"Okay. Ready?"

"Do it."

Joe removes the veil of protection that surrounds me. Magic comes rushing back into my cells, as fresh as a cold glass of water.

It's as though I've been holding my breath, and suddenly, I'm reminded to breathe. "Clauditis," I cast. The magic leaves me before I can close my mouth on the spell.

Joe works quickly, and the protection void surrounds me again.

I push the door open, and on the other side is Gemma.

CHAPTER 30

LUCI

JOURNAL ENTRY

Off the coast of the Netherlands, a song rings out into the night. A soft voice catches on the ocean waves and is carried on the fog to the passengers of The Leanna.

When I ask about the ballad, the men aboard The Leanna are wary.

"I hear a song," I insist. "Listen!"

"Rubbish," one of the men says.

"A lie the handmaids ashore made up to scare you, lass," comes from another.

"Cover yer ears!" says one who takes no chances, and he goes below deck to hide.

I don't understand such cowardice over music.

This is why women are not allowed aboard such vile vessels without escorts. We are considered untrustworthy, spouting falsehoods about such randomness as a woman's voice from the sea.

As if by mere mention, the song might sing the men of The Leanna to their deaths.

Absolute rubbish.

The storm becomes thunderous. Her song grows louder, just audible above the battering of waves on The Leanna. I strain my ears to listen.

It's lovely.

The men on the upper deck cover their ears. They drop their ropes and their bodies to the ground. They cover their heads and yell to drown out the song I know is playing angelically in their heads.

I know because I hear it, too.

It is the most beautiful melody I have ever heard, like a song from the watchful eye above. I know everything on this terrifying night will be okay. We will weather the storm to a haven.

I pick up the edges of my gown and walk to the furthest boundaries of the boat. I am careful, holding onto the ropes and the wood rails along the way, but my body still sways with the storm.

I lose my footing once.

Twice.

The song grows.

Three times.

One of the deckhands yells, "Save yourself, lass! Cover your ears."

Save myself from what?

From the music?

From the ocean?

From the edge of the boat?

My fingers wrap around the bow while my eyes venture to the ocean below. What could scare these mighty men to cower in the corners of this vessel?

Waves strike the ship, lifting and tossing us like a child's toy.

A song once light as a feather is now deep, wrapping tendrils around my insides. It is beckoning me to join the sea, to become one with it.

The closer I lean over the ship's edge to hear their call, to see them in the water with my own eyes, the more the song envelops me like a warm blanket on the coldest of nights—a hug from my mother and father, who I long parted ways with. They whisper of their love and safety. They tell me I am brilliance and light. They tell me I will be happy again if I let myself give in to the call.

To be one with the ocean's lapping waves is a pull I can no longer deny.

With both arms stretched out, the wind holds me in place, suspended in time. No longer bound by the misgivings of this world.

Movement in the sea.

A tail flaps.

I see them.

First, there is only one; then there are three.

There are more, so many more.

Fins and freedom call to me.

I'm coming home. Please wait for me.

Afraid the sea has stolen my voice, I call out, "Don't leave. Wait for me!"

I stumble but find my footing again. I climb up onto the railings, one leg at a time.

The men's voices grow louder behind me before they are gone.

Someone tugs at me, but they are shaken off by an angelic force of nature.

It is only the sea and me.

I part ways with the boat and meet the ocean.

Darkness, scales, and a deep voice carry me until I am no more.

Then, the sea withdrew.

CHAPTER 31

DAGON

Scarlet sits on the beach, her feet in the sand. She's reading the journal I gave her while slowly picking at her breakfast.

I could watch the sun dance rainbows in her raven hair forever. She holds a forkful of eggs to her lips for a long moment, caught up in the words on paper, before finally allowing the nourishment to enter her body. She sets the fork down and sips her coffee.

When she's done with an entry, Scarlet shuts the book and runs her fingers along the edge of the spine. She doesn't open it to read more. Instead, she savors the entries.

I am not so patient. I would have read it all in one sitting, devouring its content as quickly as I could.

Scarlet's ability to move at her own pace, regardless of external pressures, is marvelous. It is one of the things I've always admired about her.

It always brought a calm to my chaos.

But there's an itch interrupting my thoughts.

A crawling sensation at the back of my mind that I can't shake.

I won't shake.

Someone is watching me.

It's not the first time I've felt this sensation.

This body is limiting in so many ways. I've spent time in a variety of hosts. Usually, it's much easier to tell when I'm being followed, spied on, or when someone is using magic nearby.

But this body? This one is infuriating.

So leave.

This body would be easier to manage if you were the one who left.

There is a wall of unknowns, like an anti-magical blanket laid upon the world around it. It makes it difficult to tell when there is a foe in my midst.

Not impossible.

Difficult.

Scarlet is pouring herself another cup of coffee. I watch her soft movements with envy.

There's that feeling again.

The itch.

Slowly, I move from my chair, taking my cup of coffee as I walk the path, keeping Scarlet in my peripheral vision.

Someone is watching us.

Hunting us.

The Circle?

Her pesky friends?

They don't smell like one of mine.

Too bitter.

Not enough rot.

A breeze picks up, and the smell is gone. The unwelcome guest departs as quickly as they arrive.

CHAPTER 32

SUKI

JOURNAL ENTRY

Today, I am no longer a child of twelve. My mother says that I am now a woman of thirteen. I have familial responsibilities that I must take on.

My father has found a suitor for me. We are to be wed at the week's end.

Mother says if I do my duty as a wife, he will provide me with a fair and good life.

But I am not ready to be a wife or to run my own household. Who is going to listen to me?

Mother says she has taught me well. I am to remember her lessons and be kind to those around me. She says she will always write to me, but that I will be so busy I will not have time to miss her.

She's wrong, though.

I miss her already, and I haven't even left yet.

It was not until my wedding day that I met my betrothed.

Father wouldn't let him look at me until we were bound by law and sky.

It is the way.

My eyes are averted, my head cast down, covered by a veil, so he cannot look upon me until after the ceremony is completed. I glance at his feet and find they are large—three times the size of my own.

When all heads are bowed, I peek through the veil at his silhouette.

I gasp and lower my head further.

He is old.

I did not know how to imagine my husband. Maybe he would not be handsome. I am not so shallow that I could not love an ugly man. But I never imagined he would be older than Father.

I can feel my mother's gaze upon me, her dissatisfaction with me for looking at him before we are wed.

My heart sinks.

Familial obligation.

The weight is heavy on my shoulders and in my stomach.

I do not want to be his wife.

Or the mother of his children.

It does not matter what Mother says or what Father believes of pride and duty.

I will not do it.

The ceremony finishes, and when he removes my veil, I see him fully for the first time. He reminds me of Grandfather.

Bile rises in my throat, and I take two slow breaths to keep it at bay.

My husband takes my hand in his own and walks me from the ceremony.

When he comes for me this evening, I am ready. I am prepared to leave this life without shaming my family.

Only it isn't my husband.

It is a woman. She is beautiful, with long dark hair. Her almond eyes are soft, and when she smiles, I am taken away.

I want to look into her eyes for eternity.

Her name is Dagon. "Do you want to leave this place, Suki?"

I set my sword down and stand. I can only nod my response.

"Come with me. Let me show you there's a life worth fighting for. A life worth living," the woman says, stretching out her hand. I take it.

With a smile on her painted lips, we leave his home and never return.

She shows me how to be strong.

How to be free.

More than that, I get to live my life for me.

CHAPTER 33

MARCUS

Magic comes rushing back into me. I cast "Clauditis" and unlock the door. The magic leaves me before I can close my mouth on the spell.

Joe puts his walls up, and the protection void surrounds me again.

I push the door open, and on the other side is Gemma.

"Cessabit," Gemma casts.

But Joe is faster. He encompasses Gemma in his void, preventing any spells.

"Where's Scarlet? What have you done to her? What did you do with the vials of her blood? Where's Zig?" My words spill out in a rush.

"Marcus, give Gemma a chance to speak," Joe says. "It's the least she can do." Joe never takes his eyes off her, watching her step from foot to foot.

Gemma opens her mouth, and suddenly, her whole body lurches into the air. Her head jerks to the left, then whips to the right, and a cracking noise rings out into the room.

Gemma's body, airborne, goes limp, and she falls to the floor.

I stumble backward and into a wall, putting space between myself and her limp body. "What just happened?" I ask.

Gemma's eyes are still open.

Staring at me.

Joe goes to Gemma's side, places two fingers on her neck, and feels for a pulse. "She's gone."

"I don't understand. I thought no one could use magic in your void. How did this happen? Who killed her?" My voice trembles with anger.

I wanted answers.

"I don't know," Joe says. "There are ways to circumvent a void, but it's not easy to do. There's no one here."

I step over Gemma and move into the apartment, looking around every corner. I search the entire space but find no one.

"Let me out of the protection circle," I say. "I need to know."

"There's no one here, Marcus."

"How can you be sure?"

"The same way you know how to unlock a door," Joe says, standing up. "Let's go. There's nothing left for us here."

"Let me be sure, too," I insist. "I need to know."

Joe removes the protection, and I use my magic to search, but I still come up empty.

"There was no one else here. Not for weeks, from what I can tell," I say, defeated.

Joe sighs, "I'm sorry there wasn't more here, Marcus."

I look back at Gemma one last time. Her eyes are still open, marred with fear. "Something got to her before us."

"Something or someone," Joe says.

"But who?"

"That's the question, isn't it," Joe says, opening the door. I follow him out.

We go back to Max's.

Then, back to Mundi.

Back to Abuela.

Back to the books.

Back to square one.

CHAPTER 34

LISETTE

JOURNAL ENTRY

From the days when I could speak my mother's tongue, I spoke to the shadow world.

When it spoke back, I knew in my heart of hearts that I was never meant for the world of men. I was always born for the shadows.

Born to be a wild one.

It spoke to me of silent dreams and midnight dances. Of howling at the moon and swimming under the stars. We spoke of fears and of the most impossible things the shadow promised to prove true.

I whispered of my wild heart and being born to be me.

Of being free from the constraints of this life and its expectations.

But freedom comes at the cost of choice, it reminded me.

Wild happens when you are no longer safe to be around other people.

Safe to be around me?

It seemed like a small price to pay for the freedom to let my heart sing.

I did not understand the costs when I took the shadow man's hand.

I still do not.

The depths of those costs are too great for me to truly see. I try, but they elude me.

Someday, perhaps it will all be as Mother says, the world in balance with the life force around us. The light and the darkness weighing evenly on the scales at which we are all tried in the end.

How I might be tried when it is my turn still haunts me.

CHAPTER 35

DAGON

Scarlet snubs her nose at my breakfast soiree, not for the first time. She pours a cup of coffee and sits at the table with the journal.

"What's the point of being an all-powerful demon if I must live in poverty?" I say. "Those who choose to live a degrading existence when they have other options better have a good reason."

Scarlet sighs, "You're a snob."

"I've lived a very long time, Scarlet. I've had time to acquire both the taste for the comforts of this human existence and the accoutrements to enjoy it. I'm not going to apologize for indulging in them. Enjoy them or don't, but save your judgment for someone else," I lift the lid on today's dish.

"We traveled so sparsely before," Scarlet says, her hackles

raised. "I'm just supposed to accept the new digs, servants, and personal chef? It's weird." Scarlet throws her hands up. "Especially when you can snap your fingers and produce whatever you want. There, I said it."

I only nod at first.

"My kind of magic requires replenishment. I thought it might be easier if you had other people around." I smile. "Chef has made some of my favorites—Kajmak and beef heart tomato," I say, offering a piece of myself but knowing Scarlet will never hear it.

I fill my plate and sit across from her. "If Zig had Dagon money, would you have found it suspicious?"

Scarlet rolls her eyes.

"Enjoy the finer things while you can," I say, pouring a cup of tea for myself and digging into my breakfast. A lot of things about humans are wretched. Their food isn't typically one of them.

Scarlet fiddles with her cup while stealing glances at the journal I gifted her.

"You should eat," I say, shoveling another bite into my mouth.

"I'm not hungry."

"Have you already provided your body with sustenance today?" I ask.

"What I put into my body is none of your business," Scarlet's words are laced with anger.

"We had an agreement. If you don't like what I've provided, Chef can make you whatever you desire. But you agreed to knock off the petulant shit," I say, taking a bite of toast.

"You don't get to say what I put into my body. I know what I agreed to. I said I'm not hungry. You want to build trust? You want me to be comfortable here? You're asking a lot of me right now. So, just leave it. Okay?" Scarlet goes to stand.

I put my hands up. "Okay." I gesture to the chair and coffee. "Please, stay."

Scarlet sighs and sits back down.

A time passes before I venture, "Penny for your thoughts?"

"Why would you give this to me?" Scarlet lays a hand on the journal. "I don't understand. Some of the entries I've read have been horrific. What could you have to gain?"

"I imagine you knew it would not be all rainbows," I say.

"They don't paint you in a kind light either," Scarlet lifts her mug with both hands.

"Hmmm. I can't say much to that, now can I? It's their truth. Some of it was so many lifetimes ago, I hardly remember anymore." I sit back in my chair and think back. "I made a promise to you several lifetimes ago. I'm holding up my end of the promise."

Scarlet shakes her head. "I don't understand."

"What don't you understand?" I ask.

"How did it happen?" Scarlet asks.

"What?"

"When did you take over Zig?"

And here I thought she was going to ask if I'd ever read the journal. How did the author write it, or how did it come into my possession?

Scarlet Singer still manages to throw me for a loop.

Chapter 36

Aife

Journal Entry

Me mum said it was the fairies.

I know better.

It came from the shadow world. When he thinks I'm not watching, he comes and leaves me presents.

Acorns and ribbons at first. Later, fruits and coins. Eventually, if I wished for something, it would be in the fairy circle.

Waiting for me.

The shadows watch my movements.

Maybe he is a fairy.

But he's also a shadow.

They always know where I'll be. If I change my route or need to pick something up from town, the shadows follow from a distance, continuously watching.

I think the shadow people protect me.

There was a man once, a red soldier passing through our village, who was not kind. He had wicked thoughts. One day, he became too forward with me in town—unkind and inappropriate.

When the red soldier left, I was okay. I was safe and unharmed. But the next day, the red soldier was found dead, floating in the river.

The shadows protected me from the red soldier's wicked plans.

Mum calls me a fairy child. She says the fae protect their own.

When she says those things, I know she's telling the truth, the same way I know my own name. I can feel it in my center.

Maybe that's why Papa left.

He knew I was a fairy child and couldn't be around me anymore.

Maybe he's out looking for the real me—the one that shares this face but not my blood.

My blood is special.

The shadows have told me so.

CHAPTER 37

SCARLET

Taking measure of Zig was always easy. The way he carried himself could say more than words on a bad day and constantly on a good one.

Taking measure of Dagon is like reading tea leaves during a tornado.

It's impossible.

"When did you take over Zig?" I ask.

"I knew this day would eventually come," Dagon says, sipping the last of his tea before pouring another cup. "Does it matter?"

I want to scream and yell and shake him until he speaks, but I know that will get me nowhere. I keep hold of my coffee mug. It gives me something to do with my hands.

Just shy of throwing it at him, that is.

"Okay, I can see it does," Dagon sighs. "How much do

you remember from that first time your sentinel used their ring and shifted time backward twenty-four hours?"

I close my eyes, absolutely shaken by his words.

"How do you…" I can't finish my sentence, let alone my thought.

"Scarlet, I'm cursed to know more about you than anyone else in this realm," Dagon lets his words hang in the air.

Fucker.

Monster.

Know me better than anyone else in this realm? What in the stars above is that supposed to mean?

"How much do you remember?" he asks again.

"I don't know," I take a breath. "I was told what happened. I know what happened."

"But do you remember it?"

I shake my head.

"I didn't think so. You've only used the ring a handful of times over the last millennia."

There is no tug at our connecting cord.

No lies.

"Tell me your name is Steve," I demand.

Dagon lets out an exaggerated sigh, "My name is Steve."

There's a tug at my core.

A lie.

"Are you satisfied?"

"Yes."

"I know about each and every time the ring has ever been used," Dagon says.

I set my coffee down and steady my hands on the table. "You know?"

"Yes."

"Do all demons know?" I ask.

"No, only higher-level beings would notice. Most demons are of a lower vibration. They are none the wiser."

I can't find my words.

"Lower vibration?" I ask, unsure of what he means.

"Typical demons all live on a lower vibration. Meaning they don't know or understand true happiness. They revel in pain and suffering. Only something of a higher vibration— and in this case, a higher-level being that understands happiness, empathy, and love—would have noticed," Dagon says, sipping his tea as if he didn't just drop a bomb on me.

We sit in silence for a long time while I process the information. The pieces of the puzzle start to click together.

"Is that how you found us so quickly?" Anger rises in my chest, and a throbbing pounds in my head. "Zig said you found us quickly. He said it had to be a rat. But there was never a rat in The Circle. It was always you."

The edges of the world start to dance with black spots.

I never had to leave.

It was always a trap.

Zig.

Oh, my gods, Zig.

This is all my fault.

"I can't speak to anyone within The Circle who may or may not have been betraying you," Dagon says. "I'm not privy to all of its inner workings."

No tug.

"It's not uncommon for that sort of relationship to build over time. I can remember more than one occasion where The Circle betrayed you," he says.

No tug.

"No one fed you information about me?" I ask.

There's a tug on the invisible lifeline between us. I feel an immediate rush of guilt and relief.

"I didn't say that. I said there was no one directly connected to you," Dagon says.

Interesting word choice.

"You didn't answer my question," I say. "When did you— how long have you been Zig?"

I think of kissing Zig and finding comfort in his arms.

I think of sleeping next to him those first several nights away.

Feeling safe.

Was it all a lie?

Was it ever Zig?

Was it always the monster?

Dagon sets his tea down and finds my eyes. "After the second time shift, I safely assumed you had a new sentinel. As only a single shift is permitted for each. Unless things have changed?"

I shake my head no.

"That meant it was your young Zig. The sentinels follow a bloodline, as far as I can tell. That leaves you with limited options."

"So, you knew Zig was my sentinel? And then what?" I prompt.

"It's not hard to find someone, Scarlet. My kind are every-where. I sent out a trace, and within minutes, I knew exactly where he was," Dagon says.

"Why Zig? Why not me?"

"Because if I put out a trace on you, someone could hurt you. I wouldn't risk this life of yours on an amateur holding some kind of nonsense grudge or trying to get a leg up. Use you as leverage," he says.

His words don't make sense. I guess if he still wanted to possess my body at the time?

"So, you knew where he was," I prompt again.

"I found you in Paris."

My heart stops.

That was our first night.

"He was paying for a hotel room, and you were nowhere to be seen," Dagon licks his lips. "I could still smell you, though. I trusted you'd be back."

"I thought you were different. I knew you were different. I just," I take a shuddering breath. "I didn't listen to my gut. I made excuses." Anger boils inside me. "This is all my fault."

"Now, now, Scarlet. The world doesn't work so cleanly. Don't play the martyr. I'm the one in Zig's body."

"I've been such a fool."

"I would argue otherwise, but I get the feeling that's not what you want to hear right now," Dagon says.

"Zig should hate me," I say, trying to push down a sob that threatens to escape.

"He doesn't."

I search Dagon's eyes, but all I find are more questions.

CHAPTER 38

ZIG

I could never hate you, Scar.

You didn't know.

You couldn't have known.

I was the fool.

I let my guard down for two minutes.

It happened so quickly.

He came in, and I couldn't fight it. I couldn't push him back out. I wasn't fast enough. I was just happy you were safe.

You were with me.

I'm the fool.

This is my fault.

If I hadn't rushed us.

Pushed us.

I'm so sorry.

CHAPTER 39

AUNA

JOURNAL ENTRY

The first time I went on a hunt, it was easy.

Easier than I'd expected it to be.

Truly easier than I'd expected anything to be.

I listened to their conversations and their plans. I waited for them to strike, for it to be more than just words, exactly as he instructed.

Then I pounced.

Starting with the first man, I slit one throat, then another, draining each in turn of their life force. I removed their evil from this world.

I stopped them from committing more atrocities.

From hurting more innocents.

Using my blood, I healed the innocent. While their minds would carry the trauma, their bodies didn't have to.

Afterward, it would ache in places I thought not possible. My body was invigorated. It healed itself in a short time.

The first kill was easy.

I felt no remorse.

Evil deserved what it got.

I can't say the same about the nineteenth.

What happened to me?

Is this who I've become?

A nightmare walking alongside the shadows in human form.

If I'm even human.

I don't bleed the same as them. I don't heal the same. I don't suffer the way a human does.

I don't have the answers, but I have this gift.

The gift of the hunt.

To make wrongs right.

Maybe others would choose differently.

In another life, so might I.

I've seen too much to turn back now.

I'm not the villain of this story. Although some would argue otherwise.

They would be right to do so.

If only they were all as easy as the first.

CHAPTER 40

MARCUS

"The cleanup crew should be here in twenty," Joe says. "We can go."

"I thought nothing could work inside your shield?" I ask. "Ayúdame a entender, Joe."

"This wasn't magic," Joe replies. "Well, not the kind you're used to. This was something else completely."

"What else is there?"

"There's a world of things you don't know about, Marcus. You're blinded just like the humans," Joe says, picking through a stack of papers on Gemma's table.

"And you're just unaffected?" I roll my eyes. "The man who can't do magic sees things the rest of us can't."

"Yes."

This grabs my attention. "I'm made from magic. I would know if there was more."

Joe crosses his arms. "Do you think we could keep

anything quiet, even from our own kind, if they knew the extent to which we protect humans?"

"I guess I don't."

Joe tilts his head. "Dragons are real."

"Okay. Sure. I mean, I knew that was a thing once upon a time. They're just super rare or something. Right?" I say, jogging my memory of Abuela's lessons.

"Not so rare. Some have been domesticated, and they are spelled to look like chickens. Others are more dangerous and live in the mountains. They produce a noxious gas that kills anything within a hundred yards. Still, there are others that take human form." Joe sits at the dining room table, running his hands through his hair. "Sometimes they're hoarders, sometimes they're more domesticated and present as collectors. I once met a librarian who was a dragon. He didn't own a single book but prided himself on the rare collection he'd acquired for his institution."

I sit, unable to tell if Joe's words are sarcasm or truth.

"Azeltha said you've been researching mermaids. They also take many forms. These days, if a human encounters one, they'll likely only see a seal. But it's not the only form they take."

"Does anything present as it truly is?" I ask.

"Nothing dangerous does. It would cause too much chaos in the human world," Joe seems to measure his words. "Rarely do things that are dangerous."

"Why?"

"There are a lot of reasons. Dragons, for one, were being hunted to extinction," Joe says.

"And that's a bad thing?"

"Your abuela would be disappointed in you," Joe says, sounding equally disappointed.

"About a dragon?"

"Marcus."

"What? I'm trying to understand, but," I throw up my hands, "I don't."

"There's a lot about this world you're not ready to understand. Dragons and mermaids are only a small part of it," Joe says.

"And Gemma's death is another one of those things?"

"I knew your skull wasn't as thick as your abuela says it is," Joe says. "I don't know what killed Gemma, kid. This world has more than just witches."

"Could you show me sometime?" I ask hesitantly.

"Sure, I think I can arrange that. We need to leave, though," Joe stands, checks his pockets, and heads for the door.

We might not know what killed Gemma, but I suddenly hope to see a dragon.

CHAPTER 41

POPPY

JOURNAL ENTRY

What came first, the demon or the humans they possess?

We may never learn the truth. From my tenuous understanding, it seems most demons were once human. Their actions and belief systems in one life lead to their rebirth in the next.

The boy with the black eyes explains to me the complexities, but I often get lost in his words. Our languages are not so compatible. He is patient with me until I understand.

I do not mind the struggle.

He is the brightest point in every day. Our time together is limited. I have chores and responsibilities. But he comes every day to visit and tell me about the world outside our village. He says I am his reason for being.

I believe he speaks only the truth.

When I asked if I would become a demon like him when I

die, he told me no. I will become myself again, born to be human forever.

Like I am now.

But it's different somehow.

I asked if I would still be able to release those held captive by blood curses. He assured me I would. That my gifts carry over into each new life.

Sometimes, I wonder if he knows I can break the demon's curse. They inhabit humans and walk among us. I don't dare share this secret.

I know it is not his body he speaks from. If I was supposed to know, he would have told me.

He does not trust me the way he says.

He wears shame.

Breaking the demon's curse was accidental.

We were visiting the medicine woman in the village. She looked me over and said, "You hold a great secret, child."

I thought she was going to speak of the boy.

Instead, she spoke unfamiliar words, "Absolvisti daemonium. Ab hoc animo integrum."

When I was putting the pigs to bed that night, I saw my first demon other than the boy. Her eyes were black as coal. She attacked me, and I fought back. Blood was spilled.

I heard the witch's words in my mind, absolvisti daemonium. Ab hoc animo integrum.

I spoke the words, no more than a whisper.

Darkness poured out of the woman, leaving her limp. I thought death had come for her. But after some time, she rose again.

I have to question if everything I know to be true is but a falsehood.

Perhaps all witches aren't evil. We go to see them for medicine, but it is still a shameful act. We do not speak of the questions we ask a witch or the help they provide.

In the same breath, I wonder if all demons are not good. I thought the boy with black eyes was noble. Then, one of his own attacked me. One of his own stole a human body.

I do not know as much as I thought I did.

Chapter 42

Dagon

This time will be different. Patience will win Scarlet over. She will read the journal, and she'll finally understand. She will see all that came before her. She will remember who she is.

Scarlet will understand.

Scarlet has died by your hands more times than you can count. This time will be no different.

You're wrong.

I slip into the nearest bathroom and slam the door shut, thrusting myself in front of the mirror, and look this body up and down.

How does this feel, Zig?

Look at yourself.

Do you see me inside you? How does it feel to know you have nothing left in this world? Not even your eyes are your own anymore.

These eyes flash black. I will show him who this vessel belongs to.

You're a depraved body-snatching thief.

I sigh and smile into the mirror.

Trust is the foundation for change. Scarlet trusts me. We can change things together.

This is a new world and a new chance at a life together. Trust is everything.

Scarlet doesn't trust you. She trusts a blood-binding. That's not you, demon.

From day one, she didn't even notice you were gone. There was no difference between who she thought you were and who I am. So, tell me again how much better you know, Scarlet. Because I have known her through every life she has lived.

Do you know her wants and desires?

Do you know her fears?

She fears you.

She loves me.

She could never love you.

Let's try a simple question, Zig. Do you know what her favorite book is? What her mother's name was? What her favorite flower is? Do you know anything about her except for what you've constructed of her in your head?

These are facts. They're not Scarlet. She's more than just a stream of facts, demon.

That's where you're wrong, Zig. They are Scarlet. I've known her in every incarnation. You will never understand her the way I do.

Stop it.

How well can you say you know our dear Scarlet?

Shall I count the exact number of days you were in her life? Would that help you?

I shake my head and tsk. What kind of love is that?

This time will be no different.

I glimpse my eyes, penetrating through to the pathetic leech watching me from the inside.

I will make everything you hold dear my own if you do not silence yourself.

Zig does, although his words linger in my mind, wrapping around me like a noose.

This time will be different.

Scarlet is ready to listen.

She's ready to remember.

I leave the bathroom, his words still reverberating in my mind.

CHAPTER 43

HELENA

JOURNAL ENTRY

The stars dance across the sky. I've never seen anything like it before. I fear they might fall to the earth, but he assures me we are safe.

I am safe.

He tells me the stars are on fire, moving so fast that it looks like they are dancing in the sky.

I don't feel safe when the sky is on fire.

"Make a wish," he says.

"I don't understand. Why would I do such a silly thing?" I ask.

"When the stars dance in the sky, it's tradition to make a wish," he says.

I close my eyes tightly, and in my heart, I make a quiet wish.

"What did you wish for?" he asks.

"I wished for a life of comfort and understanding," I say.

"Your heart is still young, and you are so innocent. If you had experienced true heartache, you would have wished for something different," he says.

"I don't know what that means," I say.

He kisses my cheek, and I lean back into his arms, watching the sky light up over the ocean. He intertwines his fingers with mine, and my heart is at ease.

I am happy.

I am safe.

I am loved.

There are small moments in life I will remember forever. This is one of them.

CHAPTER 44

AZELTHA

Mors labia fontis parabolam loquuntur.

Only death's lips speak the parable of the Fountain.

When Gemma tried to speak of Scarlet, she evoked the curse.

She brought it upon herself.

For better or worse, she was warned. I made an oath to protect the Fountain. That didn't stop because she died. Kelby was reborn.

I made an oath.

Gemma could have lived a long and peaceful life. She could have forgotten about Scarlet. Pushed it out of her head. Spelled the memories away. Refused to let the past be her future.

It was a choice.

Maybe she thought I was lying.

Niña tonta.

Marcus had to keep butting in where he didn't belong. Why couldn't he let it go? He has more important things to worry about.

Clearly, he needs refocusing.

Joe might already know. I don't think he'll say anything if he does.

Joe understands that the world is more complicated than the blacks and whites of The Circle. I can't let the past repeat itself.

She could have lived a peaceful life. I can't dwell any longer on Gemma's foolish choices.

What's done is done.

Gemma chose death.

CHAPTER 45

ISHARA

JOURNAL ENTRY

When the rains come, my heart finds ease. He is resting by my side while the locals are in their homes. The rains are a symbol of fruitfulness to come—of seeds planted turning empty bellies full, of dry reservoirs running over, and clean water for all. Rain crisps the air, and everything is made better for it.

My love leans in and kisses my cheek, cradling me. He is not always patient with the world, but he always has patience for me. He is not a perfect man, but somehow, he is perfect for me.

I spent most of my life thinking I'd never find a partner who could understand me. Someone who wouldn't look down on me for being different.

For being too much.

I can't help who I am any more than a fish can help but swim.

I am a smart and kind woman, but I am still different. Being different in this world makes you an outsider. No matter how much I try, I know I will never be normal.

I am happy with who I am. But it was lonely.

When I met my love, he didn't see all the ways I was broken. He saw all the ways my parts shined. He saw my awkwardness as a strength, not a weakness. He saw me as a woman worthy of words, respect, and love.

He never saw me as anything or anyone other than who I am.

Ishara.

Queen of the Sea.

As far as partners, men, and gods go, I could have done worse.

Regarding lovers, I couldn't imagine spending my life with anyone else.

Dagon is the love of my life, and I am his.

THE FULL MOON WILL BRING THE END OF THIS CITY.

The end of us.

"You will die by his hands until the end of time."

The words echo into the night—a promise of pain and hope wrapped in terror.

Dagon smote him on the spot for speaking such a curse. The look of surprise brought a moment of relief.

The idea that Dagon could hurt me, let alone kill me, is not one I can understand.

He would never.

He could never.

Dagon would set fire to the world and let it burn before he let anything happen to me.

The man is wrong.

But the end of us will come just the same. A curse like that won't be broken easily.

If ever.

We have three weeks until the full moon. Until we are broken forever.

Three weeks to say goodbye.

Three weeks to spend with my love.

CHAPTER 46

SCARLET

There's a knock at my door, disrupting my reading. I haven't been able to think about much else but the journal Dagon gave me.

It consumes all my time and energy. Are the women real? Are their stories real?

I have so many questions.

"Who is it?" I ask before opening the door.

"Breakfast." It's Dagon's sultry voice.

I sigh and open the door.

He wheels in a cart with a variety of breakfast offerings. "It's been a while since you've had an American meal. I asked the chef to make you all the best—scrambled eggs, pancakes, French toast, bacon, hashbrowns, and some fruit."

There's also a pot of coffee. I pour myself a cup and sit down in a chair on the balcony, leaving the food behind.

"I know I'm not your favorite person right now," Dagon says.

"Ha." I nearly choke on his words.

Dagon, a person?

As if.

Dagon takes a slow, controlled breath. "Can I get you anything else, Scarlet?"

I meet his eyes, then turn back to the sea.

"Do you want to go for a tour of the island? There's much to see. I think you'd like it."

"Would I now?" I try not to spit my words, but I taste venom.

"I can see you need some time. I'll have Chef check in on you today. Farewell." Just like that, Dagon leaves.

I'm a little surprised to see him go without a fight, but I'm relieved all the same. I can't deal with him today.

When I know he's gone, I grab a fork and eat. The pancakes are like clouds. With every bite, I drift a little closer to bliss.

Not that I would tell him.

After I've eaten until I'm about to explode, I take measure of my space. I've been here a few days but have spent most of my time outside. There are floor-to-ceiling bookshelves on one wall filled with titles even I recognize. Since I'm refusing to leave my room and I've nearly finished the journal, I'll have time to peruse a bit today.

I grab the journal and crawl back into bed to finish reading the entries. To learn as much as I can about myself.

About my past.
About my beginnings.

CHAPTER 47

THE AUTHOR
JOURNAL ENTRY

My name does not matter the way these others might. Although I suppose their names are merely for legacy purposes, or they wouldn't matter anymore either.

But they mattered to me, and I thought they might also matter to you.

We are all one.

When I set out to tell the stories of Fountains from the past, I wanted to know more of myself. I wanted to understand how I became who I am today.

There is an emptiness inside of me. It is a hole that burns so deep I fear it might burn through me one day.

I have never known who to trust in this world. The Fountain before me died by her own hands. Sauvignon was a pawn in the games The Circle played.

The demons were no better, taking lives as they saw fit,

using them up, stealing innocent humans.

Did the positives outweigh the negatives?

When my sentinel passed down the necklace and I realized I could remember those lives, I knew I had to document them. If you are reading this, I imagine you will document your life much the same as I have mine.

As we all have.

I worked with a man who was a specialist in mesmerism. He helped me unlock my memories further. Sometimes, I could only remember snippets and pieces. Other times, I could recall whole incarnations.

If he thought I was crazy, he never showed it. Instead, he allowed me to simply remember.

Momentarily, I was them. It was as if their memories were my own.

I have documented them as such. They are imperfect, but I hope they do justice to our former selves.

Do you want to know my story?

For now, it's mine and mine alone. I have shared what I am willing to here.

I made an agreement with Dagon. He will pass this book on to the next Fountain, to each of us willing to read it and give it the proper time and energy. I used my life to create it. He has assured me that others will get to read it.

I do not know if I trust him with my life. But I trust in this agreement we have made. He is good for his word, but his words can be slippery.

Through this process, I have come to understand there has been enough betrayal for a thousand lifetimes. That kind of mistrust breaks a person. It leaves wounds that carry in our souls, in our blood.

Trust is beyond me now.

I hope that you are able to find trust.

I cannot tell you who or what to trust. Perhaps just yourself.

Trust that you have the answers, even if the world tells you otherwise.

Listen to your gut. It has never led me astray.

From one Fountain to another.

FAREWELL.

PART THREE

THE PRESENT

"Real generosity toward the future lies in giving all to the present."

Albert Camus

Chapter 48

Marcus

The trip home has filled me with dread. Explaining to Abuela that Gemma is dead is one thing, but also having to explain that we have no idea who killed her is a whole other kind of complicated.

The events of the day replay again and again in my mind —Gemma lurching back and forth midair before dropping to the ground.

I suppose we all must grow up at some point. Although I feel like I've done a lot of growing this past year. It seems relentless these days.

The hard stuff never gets any easier.

"Abuela?" I call out.

"Kara?" Joe says, right behind me. "We need to talk."

"You're going to wake the dead," Abuela says, rounding a corner. "A mi oficina."

We follow Abuela into her office per her request. She shuts the door and sets a protection spell.

"The cleanup crew has already been in contact," Abuela eyes me and runs a hand across my cheek. "Are you okay?"

I nod. "Yeah, I'm fine."

"Me too, thanks," Joe says.

Abuela raises an eyebrow. "Tell me what happened. They said she had a broken neck?"

I meet Joe's eyes.

"Did Gemma have any enemies?" he asks.

Abuela sighs and sits back in her chair. "We all do, Joe, you know that. No one was within your protection?"

"No one," he confirms. "Marcus, Gemma, and myself were the only ones there."

"Then it had to be one of the protected or possibly a curse? However unlikely that may be. Another demon? Maybe Gemma had loyalties elsewhere? Or did she make a bargain?" Abuela pinches the bridge of her nose and swipes a tear away.

"I'm sorry, Abuela. I—" I don't know what else to say. I want to ask what the protected are and if curses are really that strong, but I don't.

I make a mental note to research them later.

"Demons have their own loyalties," Joe says. "They're the most likely culprit. But she could have pissed anything off. Gemma left in such a hurry. If she was a traitor, she got what she deserved. If she wasn't, there's not much we can do about it now."

I can't help but feel like we're falling down a rabbit hole, one that will lead us nowhere except to a parade of more questions.

Then I think of something. "Could we pull up a hologram? Err, memory spell?" A glimmer of something out of the corner of my eye pulls my attention, distracting me momentarily.

"It would only show us a demon or a human. Neither of which were present," Joe says. "I'm sorry, Marcus, but it would provide us with nothing."

"The memory spell we used for Scarlet also showed her cat. So, we know it can show more than just humans and demons," I say. "Maybe it would show more?"

"That's not how it works. I should have been clearer, but I didn't think I had to include pets. My apologies," Joe says.

Something doesn't sit right.

There's a saltiness to the air.

"Do we notify anyone?" I ask.

"Don't worry, Nieto. I'll take care of everything. You put this behind you and get back to your studies," Abuela stands and hugs me. "Te amo."

"I love you too, Abuela."

CHAPTER 49

SCARLET

When I awaken, I'm greeted at the door with a note and a box.

Another present?

This time, there's a pair of shorts and a purple tank top with subtle beadwork.

I don't want to admit it, but I kind of love it. It's exactly what I would have picked out for myself.

I hate that Dagon knows me well enough to buy my clothes.

There should be rules against this.

It's gross.

I look through the box, expecting another puzzle, but instead, I'm met with a blank journal.

It's beautiful.

Rose gold cloth binding and paper with the perfect texture. No lines, which means more room for my sketches.

There's a fountain pen engraved with my initials, S.S., at the top.

The note reads:

Dearest Scarlet,

Please do me the honor of joining me for breakfast. I'd like to keep the lines of communication open. I noted the last time we were together that you were running out of pages in your journal. I hope you'll accept this small gift.

D

Was he reading Jensen?

I guess he could have genuinely noted that I'm almost out of pages. I honestly only have a couple left. I've been writing sparingly, trying to avoid running out before I could shop for another. With everything that's happened, it's been difficult.

I am choosing not to read into this. Instead, I'm going to accept the gift.

Probably.

Besides, why let it go to waste just to prove a point? I don't have to take it out on the book. It's not its fault.

After a quick shower, I slip on the new clothes. It's been so warm here that I feel like I move through my four outfits in two days flat. None of which are suited for this weather.

Just be open to listening to his story, Scarlet.

You don't have to believe him.

You don't have to like it.

You just have to listen.

Maybe you'll learn something new. Confirm something you've read. Or catch him in a lie.

He is good for his word, but his words can be slippery.

"I could get used to eating on the beach every day," I say, taking my seat across from Dagon.

"That could be your life. Just say so, and I'll make your dreams come true," Dagon holds my eyes, and I realize his words are more than banter.

"What's for breakfast?" I ask, avoiding his gaze.

A smile plays at Dagon's lips as he removes the lids from dishes on the table, "Grits, bakes, and saltfish fritters. I also had Chef conjure up some fruit and coffee, of course."

We eat in silence. I'm surprised at how much I enjoy the strange foods, especially the saltfish fritters.

Only when the waitstaff have cleared the table and refilled our coffee and teapots does Dagon break his reserve. "I want you to know that you're safe with me. I can sense the trepidation you carry." Dagon collects his thoughts. "I know you're worried about this body, and you're concerned about your future."

I cross my arms, uncomfortable with where this conversation is heading.

"I'm only trying to say that you're safe as long as you're by my side. No shadow will cross me without meeting a final death," Dagon says. "You have my word."

"Is that what happens when something is killed on this," I search for the right words, "plane of existence?"

"No. Not typically speaking."

Great.

Can't even kill demons permanently.

Is everything I thought a lie?

"When demons die here on this plane, they're sent back. Typically, it's not permanent, but it takes a long time to acquire passage back to the surface of this reality."

Martin brings a plate of Danishes out and sets them on our table.

"Thank you, Martin," Dagon says, reaching for a lemon one. "Scarlet?" he waves to the tray, and I grab a pear Danish.

"Thanks." I don't want to disrupt the train of our conversation. I don't know what to ask, but if I'm honest with myself, I don't know how much The Circle knows about demon passages to and from our world.

When Martin leaves, Dagon continues. "A demon can only come to earth when they're summoned. If they die, it takes a sacrifice to bring them back." Dagon sits back in his chair and watches me.

"You're saying that if a demon dies here, and no one remembers them, then they'd die permanently?"

Dagon measures the air with his hands. "That loosely sums it up. In the simplest terms, at least."

"What would happen if someone or a whole group believed a lie?" I ask.

"Ahhh," Dagon shifts in his seat.

There's an unease in my chest.

He wants to lie to me.

But will he?

"Then who you are and who you've always been becomes subject to those who win wars and write the history books," Dagon's words are cold.

A truth.

"You said a final death? Is there such a thing?" I ask.

I'm almost too afraid to know the answer.

Especially if it doesn't exist for me.

How could it be for the reincarnating girl?

"A final death is when you meet with Death herself."

"Herself?" I interrupt.

"She takes you to whatever place your soul believes you belong. Some, like our bartender who sacrificed his heart, believe in an actual Hell. I'm talking flames, being tortured by the unfathomable, and reliving your worst memories all day, every day for eternity," Dagon says. "If he didn't live up to the standards he judged others by for entering the pearly gates of the Heaven he also believes in, guess where he gets to spend his days?"

"No."

"Yep. Hopefully, he was as kind a person as the lens in which he judged others."

"Why would anyone—I mean, how come—I don't understand," my words fumble.

"The universe is powered by belief. It's more complicated than that, but in its most simplistic definition, it exists because we believe it so."

"So, if I believe I'm a millionaire, poof, I've got a million bucks?" I say, with more than a little sarcasm.

"If you believed it with every part of yourself, yes. But you won't. No one ever does." Dagon runs his hand against Zig's formerly shaved hair. It's grown longer in recent weeks. "But if you believe you're a millionaire and take action to change your life and career, you've got a good shot at making it happen."

"So, Death is a woman," I say.

"Yes, a formidable one, too."

"What would happen if someone stopped believing in death?" I ask.

Dagon shrugs. "I guess if a person truly stopped believing, they might live a long time. Perhaps this is where vampires come from. Folks who have learned to harness their magic and belief to stop Death in her tracks."

"That's an interesting thought for sure," I say. "Are vampires real?"

Dagon shrugs again. "I have lived for thousands of years, and there is still much about this world I know little about."

"If there were vampires, do you think The Circle is protecting them?" I ask.

His eyebrows raise. "I suppose it's possible. They're protecting the last of the unicorns, and I've heard even werewolves are getting a pass. Although I can't confirm, as I've never met one myself. Fae are real, though. So, it stands to reason that anything is possible."

I nod slowly, "Belief being what it is these days."

"You're catching on."

"Can you show me these things? I want to see more," I say, guilt washing over me after the words leave my lips.

"Not in this body," he says.

A mix of relief and absolute devastation.

"But someday, if you let me, I'll show you everything," Dagon says.

There is no tug, no insecurity, no lies of omission.

Just honesty.

And I don't know what to do with any of it.

A smile tugs at my lips. "I'll think about it."

CHAPTER 50

DAGON

Scarlet lets me walk her back to her room. She opens the door and nods a silent goodbye.

I wait for her to close the door before walking away, thinking of all the things I wanted to say.

If you let me, I'll show you the hidden world.

Give me a chance, Ishara, come back to me.

It can be different this time.

Do you need proof?

Should I be good? I've been good before. I can be good again.

Would you rather they burn? Trial by fire if it means keeping you.

I've waited so long, Ishara.

Let me prove myself this time.

We can break the curse if we believe together.

CHAPTER 51

ZIG

That's not true.

That can't be possible.

I would have known.

I should have known, Scarlet.

The Circle wouldn't have—I mean, they shouldn't have—

I would have known.

There was always more to my being.

Joe protects the world.

My job was to protect as well. But I wasn't ready yet. I was distracted.

I should have known.

I should have known.

CHAPTER 52

DEAR JENSEN

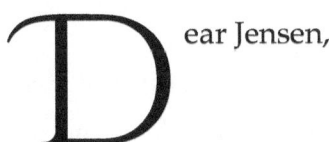ear Jensen,

DO YOU THINK IT'S POSSIBLE TO BELIEVE IN SOMETHING SO MUCH that it changes the world around you? What if we really could manifest our own realities?

Let's pretend what Dagon told me about the power of belief and its effect on reality in this life and the next is real. What does that mean?

The implications are enormous.

Questions mount in my mind, and I don't know where to begin.

I also don't know how I feel about the offers Dagon keeps

making. I understand that no offer from a demon comes without its strings.

The journal entries I've been reading are a lot to process. It seems perhaps Dagon wasn't always a demon himself? I'm not even sure when or how it might have happened.

Since the entries are only from previous Fountains, and only bits and pieces at that, I have no idea what happened when they weren't around. Not to mention, they were all written by a singular Fountain. So I don't know how exact their memories are in the first place.

One calls him a god, and another says he's a shadow. A lot of them refer to Dagon as a shadow. In fact, he's not always a man either. Sometimes, he's a she. I suppose that doesn't matter much.

It's just the face of whatever body he's inhabiting at the time. I can't imagine it was his. However, it does lead me to my next question: when did he lose his body? How long was it his face before it wasn't?

The essence of who Dagon is appears to always be the same.

I keep circling back to my question. When did he leave his own body?

When did the belief in Dagon change from god to demon?

Who changed it?

Why?

How did a collective belief change like that? Was it overnight or over years? Decades? Centuries?

Does it matter?

I'm guessing, to him, it does.

Was it malicious or a coincidence?

Maybe I'm completely wrong or absolutely off my rocker here.

I don't know. I doubt it, but still.

I'm willing to accept that there is a possibility that I've completely misconstrued this whole thing into something wildly out of line with the truth.

That's what a non-magical person would say. A human. A normy.

I miss Marcus.

He'd know what to do. And if he didn't, he'd at least have a better grasp on all this than I do. He'd tell me whether I was or wasn't crazy.

I hope, for his sake, he's forgotten all about me. That he's moved on with his life and become the leader he was always supposed to be.

If only the whole world could do the same.

That won't ever happen, though. Dagon believes in me too much. The Sentinels believe. The whispers of those who remember live on.

So, I keep coming back.

I'll always come back as long as they remember me.

That's an exhausting thought.

One I can't quite wrap my head around. I guess I don't really have to yet.

Soon, though.

Soon.

• • •

SCARLET

CHAPTER 53

DAGON

It didn't take as much convincing as I thought it might to get Scarlet on this yacht with me. I expected her to argue or try to convince me to hunt for Nameera's buried treasure alone.

But instead, Scarlet just said, "Okay."

"Okay?" I asked, hardly able to believe my ears.

"Sure."

Martin packed our things, and we set sail. We met the sea in all her glory to travel home.

Home.

I've taken Ishara to many places over her lives, but never home.

"I don't think I'll ever get used to all this," Scarlet says, a longing in her voice.

"To the water?" I ask.

Scarlet shakes her head. "To the luxury."

"I could give you the world, Scarlet. There's nearly nothing on this Earth I couldn't provide you on a golden platter," I say, not looking at her. "The grandest luxury or beauty in life's simplicity."

"You would always be a demon," Scarlet says.

"Time is relative," I reply. "Not even I can say it will be like this forever. I don't know the future. I don't think anyone does."

Scarlet glances at me.

"I wasn't always a demon," I say.

This grabs her attention. "When did you become one?"

"Don't ask me unless you're ready to hear all of it, Scarlet."

Scarlet stretches her arms and takes a deep breath, building up to a question. "Your home?"

"Is it up to your standards?" I ask.

"It's Pemberley." She bites her bottom lip.

I breathe a smile. "Pride and Prejudice was your favorite book in two lives. Maybe a third by the looks of it."

Scarlet shrugs.

"You wore out the first copy you had of Jane Austen's novel. The binding started to come apart, and you refused when I offered to fix it. You'd purchased it with your hard-earned money, which made the book so much more precious to you," I say, chuckling at the memory. "The Caribbean offers privacy, yearlong sunshine, and the ability to build whatever my heart desires. You desired Pemberley. So, I built it."

Scarlet closes her eyes.

"Are you hungry? Do you want a snack or something?" I ask, giving her an out from the conversation.

Scarlet sits there and takes in the ocean, avoiding my gaze.

She's not ready for the whole truth yet.

She may never be.

But I can wait.

CHAPTER 54

SCARLET

Dagon hints at a shared past.

If knowing some of it means knowing all of it, I'm not sure I want to know any of it. I remember enough of Kelby's life to know it was horrific.

I don't want to remember the little details if it means remembering all the darkness. Some things are better left alone.

The journal indicated there were lives that were happy and others that were equally troubling.

What if there are things that I'm not proud of?

What if those things make me more like him?

What if I'm a monster?

If I ask—if he tells me—I can't unknow whatever knowledge he shares. The good, the bad, or the ugly.

The author of Fountains past must have gone through an

absolute mind fuck trying to sort out what was. Do I trust all her words?

I don't know.

Do I trust his?

I don't know.

There was something the author wrote, though. She said to trust myself. That when I don't know who to trust in all the chaos, to trust my gut.

"What happened during the meat suit uprising?" I ask, finally breaking our silence.

"A lot. Do you have a more specific question?" Dagon asks.

"I was told it was the Underthings Network, and then it became The Circle. What changed? Why did the witches rebrand?" I ask.

"A lot happened. It wasn't any one thing. It was several things that took place," Dagon sighs. "There is this grand misconception that The Circle are the good guys and that all demons are the bad guys."

Dagon is standing at the wheel of the boat. He takes a drink from his water bottle. "It's never been so black and white. There are layers of gray. Impossible decisions are made every day. Let me ask you, does the good of many outweigh the good of one?"

I sit with his words, letting them sink in. But I come no closer to an answer. "I don't know."

"After thousands of years of making these impossible choices, a few bad ones are bound to be made. Poor leadership is inevitable; eventually, it all catches up with you," Dagon says, matter-of-factly.

It's a little surprising.

"It feels like one of those stories that could fill a library of books," I say.

"Yes, I think you're correct."

"I assume you know about the feedings?" I almost feel guilty asking, as if I'm betraying a trust, but I think Dagon knows. "You've hinted as much."

"Ahh yes, the ritual poisoning," Dagon spits his words. "Because it's not bad enough to hide the truth from the entire human race, they must also go around and kill them off via poison on the regular."

The realization hits.

Zig once told me that if I was possessed, I would have died by eating the food.

They were poisoning me.

Me.

They poison a lot of people.

Oh, my stars.

How could I have missed that?

"How does the poison only attack those possessed?" I venture.

"Magic."

"Right. Of course."

"Magic and a lack of empathy for every human and demon bound to one another," Dagon says.

"Okay." I don't know if I feel empathy for demons. Humans, sure.

Gods above, this is confusing.

"How did you learn about it?" I ask.

"When one of my kind possesses a human, they can usually read their thoughts. It's not everything; it's more like watching a highlight reel on fast-forward. You get the gist of it."

I nod.

"One of mine possessed one of theirs, read their thoughts, learned their inner workings, learned about the tests, and other things."

I feel a tug in my chest.

Not a whole truth.

It's not a lie; it's more of an omission.

A half-truth.

"There's more to it than that," I stand to stretch, hoping to make him uneasy.

"Yes. A lot more than that and many times over. Nothing in this world is simple."

Truth.

"Okay, so I have another question," I prompt.

"Anything," Dagon says.

"When I cut myself, or my birthday comes around, I put off an aroma?" I know it's not really a question, but I ask it all the same.

"You smell like roses. The sweetest, most pungent rose that ever existed," Dagon says.

My cheeks warm.

"Your perfume, carried by your blood, is one with your soul. Your essence. So, when you've been injured, it's like releasing   concentrated   airborne   drugs   into   the atmosphere."

I sit back down.

"The potency surrounding your birthday only applies through puberty. That wanes by your eighteenth or nineteenth birthday," he says.

Dagon's words make my world spin. "I thought no Fountain had lived to see twenty?"

"Who told you that?" There's an anger-laced growl in the back of his voice. "Someone is lying to you again. Whatever they have to say to support their agenda. What fool would be so arrogant as to assume they even knew?"

"I—I don't know." I think back to where I heard it and realize I read it in Kelby's journal. "It was a previous Fountain. A journal I read."

"And who told her? Because I'm here to tell you that it's a lie. I've known you in every incarnation. The oldest of you was two hundred and forty-nine."

I shake my head no. "That's—that's not possible."

"Yes."

"No, that's. That's. No. That can't be," I stutter, unable to process his words.

"Scarlet? It is possible. Especially when your body regenerates. It's one hundred percent possible."

There's no tug.

Truth.

"What's the youngest one?" I don't think I want to know, but the words have already left my mouth.

"Eleven."

My heart stops.

Just a child.

"This is a lot of information to process," I say. "I'm gonna need a minute. Or twenty."

"Take all the time you need," Dagon says.

"What about when I'm on my period? Does that blood smell the same?" I don't want to admit this was my original question.

Dagon suppresses a chuckle, "No. That's more of a copper smell. It's a typical blood smell, how anyone who's not a match might smell. It leaves no hint of something extra on you."

"Matching?"

"We can't just possess anyone, Scarlet," Dagon sighs. "As easy as it seems, it's slightly more complicated. We can only possess those with whom we have a past life connection. It's not as free-moving as The Circle implies. We can't just take anyone."

"Past life?"

"It's more than that, but yes. It could be an ancestor or an actual past life connection. Someone we've bonded with, made contracts with, etc., that sort of thing," Dagon waves his hand in the air. "But it requires a match all the same. A good match will let us stay longer in a body, while a bad match is a much shorter stay."

"Is Zig a good match?"

"Do you really want to know?" Dagon finds my eyes.

"No."

Chapter 55

Dagon

The gulls are quiet out of respect for the sea. They know I'm near, so there's respect for me too. The water is calm, and Scarlet is lulled to sleep by the gentle rocking of ocean waves.

I could watch her sleep for all my days.

The way her hair brushes along her cheek. The light rise and fall of her chest.

The way her nose wrinkles and her toes stick out from under the covers. She doesn't snore but murmurs to the people in her dreams.

Scarlet Singer, the light of this world, sleep, my dear.

Sleep.

Chapter 56

Zig

S top ogling her!

Chapter 57

Marcus

Ground zero.

Again.

Gemma is a literal dead end.

Morbid pun intended.

Dagon is still a mermaid of uncertifiable history, and I'm no closer to any answers.

Where do mermaids live? Are they everywhere? Or only in certain types of water? Are they like humans, spread wide and far? Or is it more like a rare beetle only found in one tropical location under the right conditions?

Abuela has taken me aside no less than four times to ask if I'm okay. If I'm getting out with "friends." As if I have friends.

What about Scarlet?

Did she just flee to the back of Abuela's mind, to be lost

into the nothing forever? Did she forget that Scarlet and Zig were my friends? They were my life, and they're gone.

Our only lead is gone.

"Maybe it's time you left it to someone else," Abuela says. "Get back to your training. Your studies have slipped."

"As if my studies are the only things that matter. I'm not a child anymore," I say. "I've seen too much to go back to the innocence of childhood, Abuela."

I must find Scarlet.

If Abuela won't help me do it, then I'm on my own. Honestly, it might be easier that way.

I took an oath to protect her. To have her back as her sentinel. That's on me. Abuela didn't take that oath. I did.

Azeltha would understand.

I can't abandon her when things are hard. She left to protect us all.

To protect me.

We owe her.

Scarlet ran because of Gemma. Now that Gemma is dead, maybe she can come back.

We don't have the answers yet. But if I could just get a message to her. If Scarlet knew it was safe, she'd want to come home.

Scarlet and Zig both.

I had only just learned I had a brother, and then he was gone.

This can't be all there is.

There must be more.

I can do more.

CHAPTER 58

SCARLET

When I wake, I'm alone. Dagon is sleeping, and no other souls are on board this vessel.

There's water on the horizon. Hanging off the boat's bow, I take a deep breath. The salty air fills my lungs. In the distance, something moves in the water. I watch until I swear I'm seeing spots, but it doesn't pop up again.

I could stand in this beauty forever.

A sudden surreal feeling washes over me. I'm surrounded by water on all sides as far as my eyes can see. I've never seen anything like it before.

The only thing between me and land is a demon and his boat.

Sorry, yacht.

I'm on a damn yacht.

What in the actual stars?

On the top deck, there are cushy seats. I imagine snuggling up with a blanket and napping, the ocean air pillowing around me.

Not that I'd trust Dagon for that long.

While I know I don't need a knife to protect myself, I brought the little golden dagger I made Dagon buy me. I found some ribbon and tied it to the outside of my thigh.

I'll probably just stab myself with it anyway.

I wander the ship and find it has quaint sleeping quarters. Although something about it feels claustrophobic. There's a considerable-sized kitchen, and the seating here is more luxurious than anywhere else on the boat.

White leather everywhere.

I'm not sure why, but I would have guessed he was more of a black leather demon.

There are windows that open to the sea itself and a doorway to the deck outside.

Not that I have much to complain about. It's not like I'm chained in a cage. I push down the memories of previous Fountains.

At least there's good food, plenty of it, and enough coffee to last me until New Year's.

I dig around a bit more in the cupboards and find the supplies to make some simple French toast and scrambled eggs.

"The smell of your bean water woke me," Dagon says, yawning and stretching his arms to the sky. His shirt lifts, and I glimpse his abs.

"That should be considered a good thing in most parts of the world," I say.

Dagon maneuvers around the kitchen swiftly and boils water for his tea. After the electric kettle whistles, he takes his mug and sits at the island, watching me.

I'm glad for the distraction.

"Are you ready for round two?" Dagon says. He casually sips his tea, snaps his fingers, and a tray of twenty pastries appears. He reaches for one.

Focus on the eggs, Scarlet.

Focus.

"Yes," I say, trying to hide how nervous he's making me. "How long have you been alive?"

"That's a complicated question. This time?"

"Uhh, yes? This time. Each time?" I sigh. "All of the times."

"I'm not sure when I came to be. Some things feel as if they always were. But my earliest memories are from nearly six thousand years ago."

Dagon's words settle over me.

Six thousand years.

Six. Thousand. Years.

"I couldn't die in the traditional sense, although it wasn't for lack of trying. I wanted my life to end with every passing breath when Ishara died. My purpose was lost that day. I was lost," Dagon takes a cherry Danish and pulls it apart slowly. "I found purpose again in you."

A chill runs down my back.

"Shit." I've burnt my French toast. I move the pan to the

sink and turn the water on it. After rinsing the pan, I start again.

There's a smile playing on Dagon's lips.

Fuck him and whatever he finds worthy of an obnoxious smile.

The arrogance.

Six thousand years of utter arrogance!

Tension in my body sends heat from my chest down to my belly. I want to smack him.

I add more butter to the pan, dip my bread in the egg batter, take a deep breath, and say, "Go on."

He clears his throat. "Another three thousand years passed before my time came, as it does for all gods eventually. It lasted a few short years before the rise of a belief so strong it wiped thousands of years of history away. The use of my name but three times in a book believed so vehemently birthed me into a world where I am this," Dagon stretches his arms out, looking at himself.

He snaps his fingers, and his clothes change from a loose-fitting white shirt and a pair of tan-colored shorts to a hot pink four-piece suit. Dagon spins around. "It's a cool party trick. Definitely couldn't do this as a god," he says. Dagon snaps his fingers again and changes back.

Dagon grabs another pastry and shoves it into his mouth. "Or pulled these from thin air," he swallows. "Being a demon has its perks. They don't outweigh what I had, though."

"Belief," I can barely get the word out.

"Is a powerful thing," Dagon finishes. "As belief wanes,

so does what it created. When the fundamental story changes, so do we."

I take my breakfast off the stove without burning it this time. I sit next to him at the counter and sip my coffee, searching for the words to my questions.

"You said you were a god?" I ask, disbelief thick in my voice.

Demon, sure.

God?

I shake my head, trying to push past my distrust in him. Trying to remind myself that there was no tug of lies.

"Yes, I was a god of many things for thousands of years," Dagon says, sipping his tea.

No tug. He's just being coy.

"Like what?" I ask.

"The sea."

And the puzzle pieces click.

"Agriculture, fertility, fish," Dagon says.

"It's all making sense," I say.

"Is it?" He grabs another pastry, this time a pear one. Clearly, he doesn't have to worry about his waistline either. Or he doesn't care, because it's not his.

Dagon really brings out the venom in me.

I blow out a breath. "Tell me about Djinn," I say.

Dagon chews. "They were once a free species, like you and me, relatively speaking. Djinn were summoned by charms and spells, drawn out of hiding and their normal lives with gifts and favors. They would exchange wishes for specific rituals or if you helped them. So, you would have to summon one with a gift or a favor, and then the wisher would need to do a second ritual or favor for a wish. Djinn are extremely particular. While many of them are not fond of humans, there are others who think it's fun to play among the human realm. Since Aladdin, they are all bound and cursed to live in bottles. They grant wishes to those who possess their cages."

"The Mouse changed Djinn?" I ask, a bit flabbergasted.

"I mean, eventually, I'm sure, but I meant Aladdin and the Magic Lamp. A story written a mere three hundred years ago has reformed the Djinn way of being," Dagon reaches for another pastry. This one I'm less familiar with. He finishes his tea and pours more before taking the first bite.

I feel a tug at my chest. It's not a tug of deceit but instead one of omission.

"What aren't you saying? Who wrote the story?" I ask. Admittedly, I only know the Robin Williams version.

Dagon smiles. "It was payback. Belief is cruel. I met a young sir who wanted to share his story of Aladdin and a Djinn. After carefully reworking his story, I've provided him more than three hundred years of success."

"Wow. For a man upset about how belief has royally screwed him over, time and time again, you were sure willing to cage a whole species—did you call Djinn a species?" I wave my hand away. "No matter—you were going to cage all of them into little lamps just to seek revenge on one person?"

"They aren't human. And yes, I did. A lack of empathy for folks who don't deserve it is an ongoing battle I struggle with." Dagon sips his tea. "You won't get an apology from me, so don't bother."

"When do we make land?" I ask.

"We don't," Dagon says.

"What?"

"We never came here for the land. We came here for the sea."

CHAPTER 59

DAGON

Scarlet wears each of her emotions on her face. She doesn't hide them like most people do; instead, she moves from one to the next as she feels them.

When she's surprised, she's never able to play it cool. Her eyebrows raise, and her eyes grow cartoonishly big. When she's truly caught off guard, her nose flares, and her ears twitch.

When she's sad, it's not that she's always somewhere else, but it's more like she never entirely focuses on the things in front of her. She's always looking behind her.

Waiting.

When she smiles, she doesn't just take my breath away; she could literally change someone's life.

It's exquisite.

When she's arguing and being a general spitfire, there's an energy that runs through her veins and rises with each breath of her chest. It seeps out of her like an open spigot and pulses into the air.

Scarlet hunted with that kind of fury and passion. She was a force the world reckoned with. Anything that crossed paths with her was at the mercy of her judgment.

The venom that lies beneath her surface is intoxicating, only equaled by the healing nature and kindness she shows strangers.

Scarlet would ask herself what she needed to be at any given moment. Then, she'd ask herself what she had to do to accomplish her goal. Whatever it was, I could watch her transform before my eyes.

Scarlet is both terrifying and deeply moral.

My love is a force to be reckoned with, just like Scarlet Singer is.

She will remember.

CHAPTER 60

ZIG

The bond between Scarlet and Dagon works both ways. It took me a long while to realize it, but I can feel her now.

She hasn't outright lied to Dagon, but she omits things, just as I assume he does with her.

She's coy.

Sometimes, though, she feels things—things that can't be true, things that must be a lie.

All the lies.

The Circle.

Dagon.

Joe.

The lies never end; they just grow, becoming enormous beasts.

I don't know what I'll do if I ever get out of here. I can't go back to the way things were.

I know too much now.

Even if half of Dagon's words are false, that still leaves half of them true.

Scarlet looks at him with a mix of wonder and rage.

She feels for him—anger and a softness that she once felt for me.

It mingles, confuses her.

It confuses me.

I don't want to believe what he's saying, but how can I ignore it anymore?

CHAPTER 61

SCARLET

Dagon cleared breakfast with a snap of his demon magic-laced fingers. Where we're headed, only he knows.

"Are you ready for that story yet?" Dagon asks.

"You've taken me to the middle of the ocean. For all I know, you're really bringing me here to feed me to the fishes." I toss my hands in the air. "Sure, I guess now is as good a time as any."

"I brought you to the middle of nowhere, but I won't be feeding you to the fishes." Dagon tilts his head. "Probably."

"So comforting," I say, rolling my eyes and wishing I had something to do with my hands.

"Ishara was a lightmaker," Dagon says.

"Ishara was an entry in the journal," I think back to the pages on her.

Dagon nods. "I didn't know for sure, but I assumed there would be. She was the first, so it stands to reason."

"You're saying you really never read the pages in the journal? Any pages?" I ask skeptically.

"Never. I made a promise, and I don't break my word."

"Okay," I say, measuring his words. I have this urge to tell him everything I've read about her, to read it to him myself. But I want to hear his story first.

His words.

"You go first," I say.

"Ishara was already four and twenty when we met. Already considered old and an unmarried burden to her family."

Twenty-four doesn't feel so adult these days. Let alone married or with children. Way too much, too fast. My mom would say, *Babies having babies.*

I can't even see to next week.

"Ishara was the balance our followers deserved," Dagon looks to the sea, remembering. "She was devoted to the humans, having been one herself once."

"You, a god of the sea, married a human? Do tell, because I'm genuinely curious," I say.

"It's not forbidden and perhaps more common than you might initially think. The human must face a trial of three before being presented the opportunity to become a god or goddess themselves." Dagon brings his story back to me and smiles. "She was a lightmaker. She could bring out not just the best in those around her, but her gift was that of love."

I tick off the questions on my fingers. "Trial of three? She had the gift of love?" I don't know if that's supposed to be a metaphor. For every answer, my questions double.

"In short, yes. The trial of three tests all humans who wish to level up, as your kind might say. Ishara faced it head-on, knowing that if she failed, the consequences would be life-altering," Dagon finds my eyes. "Death of someone, herself or a loved one almost certainly. Loss of limb or soul, quite likely. The trials are only for the true of heart."

"Ishara was moral and true of heart?" I ask.

"And so much more," Dagon sighs. "Ishara was the goddess of passion, of sexuality, of desire, and marriage. She was the goddess of love. She was imbued with light from the stars. Ishara was an unstoppable force with a healing energy that touched everyone she spoke to."

I've never seen Dagon so passionate about anything but unaliving someone. It's nice to know that he's capable of more.

Maybe it means I'm capable of more, too.

"In the book, it said that someone cursed Ishara to die by your hands until the end of time," my words are quieter than I intended.

Dagon nods slowly, and it's a long while before he answers.

There's a longing in my chest.

In his.

"It was so long ago, but I'll never forget his face. When I close my eyes at night, his is the one I see. His words on repeat. No amount of time would ever have been enough with Ishara. I burned the village to the ground while I hunted him. When I found him, I ripped out his tongue first, slowly cutting the muscle millimeter by millimeter. I took my time pulling his teeth. I fed his bones to the sea, and she withdrew from me," Dagon's voice morphs into a growl.

A shiver runs down my back. Not a single pull from our internal rope.

All truth.

"Ishara would be worshiped for a long time. You can't kill a goddess so easily. But she was no longer mine. Her soul was gone. She was my Ishara no more."

"Was she a shell of a person? Or someone else entirely?" I ask, unsure.

Dagon turns and slowly walks to the boat's helm, and I follow. Once we're moving again, he turns to me. "Human souls go to the underworld when they pass on from this life. Ishara's human soul went to the underworld, too."

"Like Hades?" I'm racking my brain, trying to remember how much I know about underworld gods.

"Depends, but sure. If you believe in Hades, I'm sure you'd meet him in the underworld. Or Hel, or Jesus, or any other deity you want to name. In Ishara's case, I knew she would be with Ereškigal, the queen of the underworld and goddess of death."

"Are you saying what I think you're saying?" I ask.

"What do you think I'm saying?" Dagon raises an eyebrow.

"Sorry, go on."

"The underworld was nicknamed The Land of No Return. Ereškigal is not a woman to trifle with. Disrespecting her could mean going to the land of no return quite early and painfully. She was not only the goddess of death but was also occasionally known for bringing death to those who simply angered her," Dagon says.

"Note to self."

"Indeed."

"What happened to Ishara's soul?" I ask.

"I went to the underworld to find her. She'd been parted with her mind, her light, and her grace. I had to put her pieces together again. I had to push her back to Earth where she would fall, only to be born again."

I'm on my feet and shaking my head before I can sort out my words. "I don't understand. You put her pieces together again. You put her pieces together. HER."

"You," he says.

My whole body is trembling.

"Some part of you knew. Understood already, Scarlet," Dagon is reaching for me, but I back up.

"No, that's not possible. First of all, there's no way that I'm your long-lost dead wife reincarnated for the five-hundredth time. Second of all, you told me you put my pieces back together again. That I still had my grace. Which, for the record, is really fucking contemporary of you, especially considering you're a god of the sea. Third of all," I shove my fingers in his face in a fit of anger and fear. "I'm not—"

Dagon cuts me off. "Your mind forgets every time you are reborn. That necklace helps you remember, but it only does so much. When I pushed you to Earth, your memories were lost. But I knew I could help you remember if given a chance."

I'm shaking my head firmly. "No, I can't hear this right now."

"Okay," and with one word, Dagon is quiet.

The sea laps at the boat, and after ten or fifteen minutes of silence, my body calms.

My heart slows to a normal rhythm again.

Dagon exhales, and I stiffen. "Did I tell you I was a mermaid?" he says.

CHAPTER 62

DAGON

The sirens call my name.

The sea wraps her tendrils around my being, and I know I can't put it off anymore.

I could keep Scarlet in the middle of the ocean forever. I could devise a thousand reasons why we can't go back. I could sustain us and provide whatever she desires here at sea.

She would be here.

With me.

Eventually, she would listen.

The day would come, and she would want to listen.

They sing to me, the voices from the sea. A lullaby calling me back to my home. A place I can never truly go again.

With every breath I take, they pull me closer to the edge.

Closer to oblivion.

The constant reminder of all I've lost is exhausting. And Scarlet just pushes me away.

"Tell me about being a mermaid," Scarlet's eyes twinkle with a mischievous air.

I close my eyes, breathing deeply. The salty sea air hits my nostrils, taking me to a place that lives in the deep recesses of my soul.

I begin my story.

The sea is reverent.

A goddess in her own right.

When you live among her, you respect her. When you depend on her for life and limb, you bow to her, and she cares for you. The sea provides.

Of all the beings in this vast world, she chose me as one of her protectors.

A being made with the torso of a human and the lower extremity of a fish. Never had someone been made so strong or fast as Dagon, god of the sea.

With every passing breath, I miss the comfort and safety she provided me—food, shelter, friendship, and even love.

My time within her was sacred.

Land days were the worst. Subjugated to humans and their bigotry, petty arguments, and small-mindedness. They are infantile and torture to be around.

Until I saw her.

Ishara was the daughter of a farmer. She apprehensively

approached the temple, laid down a stack of beautiful roses, and fell to her knees. She begged my name and the stars above for her family's crops to grow.

Until that moment, I'd never inhaled the aroma of roses. It was the most intoxicating thing I'd ever encountered in my long life.

Ishara was intoxicating.

In time, I won over her heart and affection.

When we married, Ishara pushed me to become a better man and leader of the people. She dedicated herself to the humans. I was better with a goddess of love by my side. Everything was better because of her.

Our home was a masterpiece of the sea, a coral castle built by the ocean herself. On land, we moved among the humans as one of them. Humble in our clothing and possessions, Ishara was never without her roses.

PHANTOM LIMB SYNDROME IS A WICKED BEAST. THE ACHE I FEEL for my tail is haunting. The place it ought to be physically hurts. I would cast myself to the sea forever if it would bring it back.

Open water.

Never the feeling of cold again.

I miss my gills, too. Breathing like a human is so tedious. It gets old and tiresome.

These options were ripped from me long ago. Without my say. Over petty human disputes.

Now, I'm trapped in this body, trading souls for a chance at a glimmer of a memory of what it meant to be free.

So, no. Before you ask, my empathy for humans is null. They've taken everything from me—the sea, my love, my life. Then dared to trap me in this hellscape for all of eternity.

CHAPTER 63

SCARLET

Regardless of the warnings, Pandora couldn't resist a peek inside the box. After everything I've learned, I understand the need because neither can I.

"Why did the Djinn owe you?" I ask, knowing full well I can make assumptions all day, but hearing it from the demon's mouth is different.

Dagon chooses his words carefully. "When no one was left to believe in her, I lost Ishara."

The daylight has waned, and the ocean takes on an orangey tinge. Looking at him when he speaks is hard, but I asked. I need to know the truth. I turn from the sea and face Dagon.

"They rewrote Ishara's history. Cursed her to the heavens above. You weren't supposed to be one of them. You were never supposed to be a human. They ruined us!" Dagon snaps, and I draw back. "They took you away from me. I asked the Djinn to bring you back to Earth. I brought your parts together for him—blood of someone you loved, an artifact that belonged to you, the soul of a lover."

My heart leaves my chest at his words.

The soul of a lover?

Whose soul?

His soul?

"The Djinn was supposed to bring us together, but he gave you a half-life instead. Cursed you to a human existence."

"I thought Nameera was a woman?"

"She is."

I shake my head, not understanding his words.

"Tamer was her lover. He cursed you to human life. He cursed you to an eternity as the fountain of youth. When I saw and understood what happened, I attacked him. I brought forth the curse in which you died by my hands. I set it in stone that day." Dagon wipes a tear.

There are no words I can offer. My insides are a twisty mess, unsure of what to feel.

So, I listen.

"You weren't trapped in their void anymore. It didn't make it right, though. I did everything he asked. But Djinn can't be trusted. Ever. They twist your wishes and use them against you for fun. My loss was entertainment for Tamer. He laughed at my pain," Dagon spits his words.

"Why Nameera?"

"Revenge."

"Revenge?" my words get stuck in my throat.

"He took everything from me. I've spent the last six thousand years taking everything from him. I can't kill a Djinn, but I can make it so he feels a fraction of what he's made me suffer," Dagon says.

"So, you helped change their story. Now, Djinn require a bottle. A cage. And Tamer's partner has been trapped for three hundred years without one," I say. "Unable to leave wherever you've left her. Tamer unable to save her."

"Yes," Dagon says without emotion. "I will live forever. I play the long game."

"I can see that," I say.

I pace the deck, trying to understand. Trying to wrap my head around the idea of eternity. Of Djinn and of life outside of this one.

Of a hatred so deep that six thousand years of revenge isn't enough.

Of a life before this one.

After this one.

"Why would you possess me? If you think I'm your wife from lives ago, why would you do that to me?" The words tumble out of me before I realize I've said them.

I've thought of them a thousand times. Wondering if he cares as much as he claims, why would he ever consider it?

How could it be an option?

"Why do you do anything?" Dagon growls.

"Excuse me?"

"I asked you—her—them so many times. To listen. To give me a chance. I tried to reason. The witches get involved, and, in this body, with this history, you only ever see what they wrote. You only see the demon in me." Dagon closes his eyes and takes a deep breath.

He looks like he wants to throw things and light the world on fire.

"Ishara only saw the good. When you're accused of being evil enough times, eventually, it's easy to lean into it. Do the things they accuse you of. Why not? I'm being punished for it either way. Especially when The Circle is at the helm. Fuck them," Dagon says.

"When I was gifted a sentinel by a witch, it changed things for you again," I say.

Dagon nods. "You were able to take your own life then. It is so much cleaner when you could unalive yourself. The rage that boils my blood at the audacity of those absolute manipulative monsters." Dagon's fists clench and unclench.

"You taught Fountains how to hunt humans," I say.

"Revenge."

I nod. "There were several who wanted to hunt them. They were so angry I can feel it bubble inside me even now."

Dagon looks up.

"Not in every life. But in enough of them. So much anger at what's passed. You're not alone in that."

Dagon holds my eyes, and I think, for the first time, true honesty has passed between us.

CHAPTER 64

DAGON

When you decide what's best for someone, strategically choosing what to tell them or what to hold back to avoid hurting them, not giving that person a choice, it's all a form of control, Dagon. Strategic lies are a form of control. Regardless of the intentions, they are still harmful.

Ishara's words play in my mind.

Absolute honesty is the rawest form of giving up dominion over another person. Offer someone your vulnerability and truth. Not just your version of the truth, but the whole and honest truth. Let them make up their own mind. Let them be the judge with the entire picture before them. Their actions will reflect their humanity and yours.

Ishara was always honest with me.

Honesty is all I can offer Scarlet.

It's all I have left.
Honesty is enough.
It has to be.

CHAPTER 65

ZIG

All this talk of honesty.

What about me?

What about this body?

There's no honesty in what you've done to me, in stealing my life.

In refusing to leave.

There's no honesty in that.

Chapter 66

Marcus

One by one, The Circle's council members fill the tall, wooden-backed chairs around the ornate breakfast table at Max's. They pop into their assigned seats, and I'm hit with the smell of marshmallows. The taste of warm butter fills my mouth.

Worry and anxiety.

Awesome.

I have just enough time to roll my eyes before I'm hit with lemons, the unavoidable sharp taste of impatience. As if we don't have other things we'd rather be doing.

Another pops in, and the air grows thick. Sorrow makes it hard to breathe, as if I'm suffocating with lungs full of air.

Another, and I'm back to sniffing marshmallows.

It goes on this way until the table is filled, and the quiet chatter becomes static. I keep my walls down. If someone is hiding something, I want to know. Which means I'm flooded by everyone's emotions instead of selectively choosing who to read.

As always, before the meeting gets to brass tacks, everyone eats. It's a good thing because I'm starving. As soon as the food appears, I fill my plate with all the usual suspects and dig in. It helps distract me from the parade of reckless emotions coming at me.

Plus, I like food.

These meetings have never been what I would describe as enjoyable. They're necessary.

It's work.

It's not even work I'm compensated well for, but that's a whole other conversation. One Abuela would only smack me upside the head for bringing up. Especially at a council meeting.

The members have become more tense since Zig's disappearance. There is so much I didn't know about this world, between what's hidden and what's unsaid.

I don't know who to trust anymore.

Even Abuela's been hiding stuff.

"Given the situation, we need to consider all of our options," Abuela says to the table.

"We need to respect the family lines," says Edgar, the council member for Western Europe and Gemma's replacement. "Respect tradition."

"No. I refuse to exclude anyone with potential as a Void because of bloodlines. Get with the times," Mateo says, slamming his hands onto the table. Edgar sits back in his chair. "Tradition be damned. We're at war, Edgar. I'm sorry if you missed some stuff joining us so late. Take a look around. We can't afford to make mistakes."

Kenji raises a hand before speaking, "We have a Void who needs guidance. I believe they can offer a lot to The Circle. I offer them for the betterment of everyone."

"Thank you, Kenji," Abuela says. "I accept your Void. We need to be working together. Every Void needs the same level of training, regardless of who they represent or where they come from. Regardless of which family they are born to. Magic is magic."

"Magic is magic," reiterates Raja, the representative from the Middle East.

"Magic is magic," says Tayla of South Africa.

Others join the group agreement, muttering, "Magic is magic."

Someone mutters Scarlet's name, but a privacy bubble goes up, and the whispers are kept secret from me. The potential destruction she holds in her body still scares them.

"We should have never let that girl into The Circle," Zvi, the representative of North Africa, says. "I still stand by my original vote. We should have taken care of her when first presented with the problem."

"You mean murder," I say flatly. "You wish you would have just killed Scarlet."

Zvi shrugs, "Would it be better if she were possessed?"

They're afraid of me, too.

Afraid of what I'll do or sacrifice in her name. They're scared that if I must choose between The Circle and Scarlet, I won't choose them.

If they only knew.

Mateo stands. "We're not going down this rabbit hole again. What's done is done. We can't change the past. We need to look forward and stop looking to place blame."

Zig leaving his post is bewildering and beyond their comprehension. Was it love, or was it the Darkness? A demon possession or the foolishness of youth?

Nothing is safe or sacred.

Their world was upended.

I listen to these leaders talk and realize something for the first time. Scarlet was never really safe with The Circle. Not the way I thought she would be. Not the kind of safety she deserves. They see her as a threat instead of an ally.

I didn't understand the danger she was in by saving us or by protecting herself. Something we should all have the privilege of doing.

But not her.

Not Scarlet.

She made the right choice by leaving The Circle.

I feel that now.

I just don't know what that means yet.

The Circle is the only home I've ever known. There are so many lies. I'm starting to understand why Scarlet couldn't trust anyone.

I worry she'll never be safe again.

Not here with The Circle.

Not with anyone.

CHAPTER 67

DAGON

The stars above shine a pattern in the night sky that guides my way to the Djinn's secrets. Maybe it's magic or a promise from contracts of lifetimes past. But I trust the stars the way I trust the sea.

The siren's call refuses to desist and cannot be avoided much longer. It only grows with each passing moment. It started as a hum in my mind, but now it vibrates in my blood.

For some, it might be overpowering, controlling, and even all-consuming—the feeling where your whole body buzzes just before knocking on Death's door.

For me, it's pure ecstasy.

Scarlet is fast asleep. I watch her gently breathing, wishing I could capture this moment for eternity. Wishing I could pause time and carry her into a future free of this curse.

Free of the things I did to her. However well-intended they were at the time, I still failed.

Mistakes were made.

Maybe I'm wrong, but I think she's listening. I think, for the first time in a long, long time, she sees me.

Maybe Ishara was right.

I lay a soft kiss on Scarlet's forehead. Her black hair falls gently across her face. She is the embodiment of roses, and I inhale her, holding on to this moment before moving to the boat's stern.

I drop the anchor.

Removing my clothes, I reveal myself to the sea. She knows all my secrets, my scars, and my broken hearts. The sea calls, and all there is left to do is heed her.

I set a timer on my watch for thirty minutes. It's not much time, but it is all I can take. If I take too much time with her, Death will come to meet me again.

Funny how the deals we make in a moment haunt us an eternity later.

Life for a life.

The sea to breathe again.

I'm not ready to answer Death's call.

I can't go back in time.

Only forward.

Standing on the boat's edge, I set my watch and release myself to her wild ways.

The ocean swallows me whole.

I feel her move through my body, changing me, inch by painful inch.

Ripping me apart and making me new again.
Making me, me again.

CHAPTER 68

SCARLET

My dreams are shattered by a scream. My heart thumps. There's a moment where I forget where I am, who I'm with, and everything I've become.

It's dark outside.

I hang my head out of a window and take in a breath of fresh air. The ocean is serene. It sparkles, and its beauty is only matched by the Milky Way above.

"Dagon?" I say, but the room doesn't answer.

I get up and walk the length of the space. It's just as empty as I thought.

Such a strange dream, like a pull to nothing that ripped through all my thoughts.

I walk the vessel's length, but I don't find Dagon. Instead, I'm met with a pile of clothes. "He wouldn't have jumped. That would be suicide, right?" I say to the sea.

She doesn't reply at first, keeping her secrets to herself.

Then I see something. It flips in the air before diving back under the surface.

A whale?

A dolphin?

No, no, no.

Transfixed to the spot, waiting for something to show itself, I hear the ocean sing. It's soft at first, a gentle call that could be mistaken for the wind.

Until it grows forceful.

Another flip in the sea, and I know it's not a whale or a dolphin this time.

But it was a tail.

Louder, she calls for me to jump. She calls for me to get closer, just a little at first. Then maybe I could see the wonders she holds.

A shimmer of sparkles.

"Hello?" I say, asking the sea if she is real.

"Hello," it echoes back.

The voice is an unexpected caress.

"This isn't funny. Who's there?" I say.

"Whoever you want us to be," it says in return.

I drop to my knees and hold the railing for dear life, knowing that whatever magic was at work was beyond my understanding.

"It's okay, Scarlet. You're safe with me," it says.

I look inward, wondering if I feel threatened. Do I feel afraid?

I know I should be afraid, but I feel a calm move through me.

"Come closer, dear one," it says.

I move to the edge of the boat, and I lean closer.

Another tail flicks in the sea, a shimmer and sparkle catch my eyes, and there's something more.

It's so close I reach out to touch it.

But I'm still too far away.

"It's okay, Scarlet, you're safe with me," it says. "Trust us, one more step, and you'll be free."

"Who are you?" I ask one more time.

"Come see," it says.

I nod, "Okay."

Then I let go and jump.

I give myself over to the sea.

CHAPTER 69

MARCUS

S carlet stands at the bow of a boat, her arms wrapped
around herself.

She steps to the edge, transfixed.

The ocean rises to meet her.

Something is on the precipice, reaching for her.

It grabs Scarlet's arms and drags her over the side of the
boat.

A tail flaps, and both are gone.

I shake my head to clear it.

That wasn't a dream. I wasn't asleep. I look at the pile of
books at my desk and wonder if I fell asleep briefly or if it
was a premonition.

I need to help her.

My stomach hurts, like the tether to her is ripping my
insides apart.

"Azeltha!" I nearly scream into the empty room, knowing

that somehow, she's always listening these days. She's got an ear everywhere, constantly aware of what's going on.

Magical spyware, I know it.

"No need to yell, Marcus," Azeltha says, appearing out of thin air.

"It's Scarlet. We have to help her. She's—something's wrong. Someone or," I shake my head, not really sure what I saw. "Something's taken her out to sea. I think she's going to drown. Or is she drowning now? I don't know, but she's not safe."

Azeltha takes in my words but doesn't move. She blinks and sighs.

I need her to move.

I need her to show some level of urgency.

But she's giving me nothing.

"Did you protect Scarlet from Gemma?" I ask.

"I protect the Fountain, no matter the cost," she says.

"And now?"

Azeltha sighs. "No matter the cost." She leaves in a shimmer.

All I can hope is that Azeltha saves Scarlet in time, finds her. If Azeltha knows where Scarlet is—that's a line of thought I'm not ready to explore.

No matter the cost.

If Scarlet is safe, that's all that matters right now.

CHAPTER 70

DAGON

Sucking the ocean into my lungs and breathing it back out is a marvelous feeling. It's been exactly eight thousand seven hundred and eighty-one hours since I've felt the ocean move around me.

Move through me.

Thirty minutes a year is never enough.

I have little interest in meeting Death again so soon, no matter how sweet she is.

Beneath Caribbean waves, a treasure concealed. A lamp of magic, by water's grace, revealed. Emerald depths unveil my watery lair; I am the Marid of oceans with ethereal flair. Grasp the lamp, its glow in hand. A wish fulfilled by sea and its strand. In this sacred space, Caribbean's secrets are a goddess's home, found only in the ocean's embrace.

The Djinn's quest is within my grasp. I've solved her

riddle. I'll trade her the answer for a second chance at this life.

A body of my own.

A real opportunity to make things right with Scarlet and prove I am capable of kinder things. A chance for her to understand everything that's passed.

My eyes adjust to the darkening water, knowing what's concealed lies ahead.

So close.

I check my watch. It reads twelve minutes have passed.

Twelve of the most glorious minutes.

I loop in the water, knowing I have time to play. Time to enjoy every single moment. I go faster to feel the rush of water on my body.

"Come close, dear one," a song rings out and reaches my ears.

No. Everything in me goes cold. I stop swimming.

"All your dreams and wishes," they offer.

NO! I double back as fast as I can.

"Just jump," they say.

If my blood could run any colder, it would be ice. The Sirens have found her.

She was sleeping.

She was safe.

"Jump."

"Jump."

"Jump."

Chapter 71

Scarlet

Falling over the edge.

    Air.

    Sinking into the darkness.

Let us take you.

Slowly fading, becoming one with the sea.

A golden dagger sinks past me into the deep.

Soon you will be free.

I watch the glimmer of gold until the darkness takes it.

The siren's call is inebriating.

Breathe us in, Scarlet.

So, I do.

CHAPTER 72

DAGON

The ripples in the ocean communicate everything. They speak of fear and Scarlet's imminent death, but also of laughter and fun.

Sirens.

I can measure her distance in the ripples.

I can save her or get the lamp, but I can't do both with the time I have left.

The water talks and counts down the moments Scarlet has remaining.

Tick tock.

There's only time left to save the future I want.

The future I need.

CHAPTER 73

SCARLET

Coughing and sputtering up salt water, the pressure eases from my chest, and hands roll me over.

I'm alive.

Dagon holds me on my side as I continue to clear my lungs. My ribs and chest ache as if I've been hit by a truck. A hard, wet thud on the wooden floor of the boat pulls my attention. "You have Zig's torso, but you have a tail?" I say, not really meaning for it to come out as a question. I clear my throat and take him in.

Dagon is sitting on his hip, a large mermaid tail at the end of his naked body. I'd pinch myself, but I'm pretty sure I just died and came back to life.

"Yes, for another," Dagon looks at a watch on his arm, "six minutes, I'll keep my mermaid form."

"Did you get the item from the Djinn?" I ask.

"How did you know?" Dagon asks.

"I'm not dumb; I can puzzle out why we're here and parts of that riddle as much as the next person," I say.

"No, I didn't. You needed me," his voice is thick.

"Go," I say.

"There's not enough time," Dagon says.

"You saved me?"

Dagon runs a palm over his shimmering tail. There's a dark rainbow pattern to it.

"Why? Why did you save me? You could have had your Djinn. Your revenge. A body of your own. I don't understand," I say. "Why did you bother?"

"Faced with life on this planet without you again, I'd rather not wait another hundred years," Dagon never looks away from his tail. He continues to brush it gently with his palms, admiring it.

"You saved me," I say, my voice hoarse, still in shock at the truth.

"Don't let it go to your head," he says.

"You're a mermaid. It was all true, wasn't it?" I say.

Dagon inhales deeply and nods. "All of it."

"A sea god cursed to live without fins for eternity." Dagon meets my gaze.

"But your tail?" I ask.

"Right," he says, brushing it again. "I left that part out. They can take me from the sea, but they can never take the sea from me."

"I'm still confused," I say.

"Once a year, I can join with the ocean and my tail again.

It is short-lived. Through trial and error, I've learned that Death shows her beautiful face after spending more than thirty minutes in the sea. As lovely as she is, I do not need her to come for me yet."

"You can't be in the sea at all?"

"Never."

"Or," I gesture to his mermaid tail.

"Correct."

"And Death is a woman who shows up to collect?"

"Yes," Dagon smiles gently. It's a forgiving smile, one of acceptance.

"I heard a song," I say. "It was the most exquisite thing I've ever heard." Tears spill down my cheeks.

"It was the sirens' call," Dagon says.

"You saved me instead of saving yourself?" I ask, almost unable to believe this night.

"Yes."

CHAPTER 74

DAGON

The indefatigable fight to acquire a body goes on. Without the bottle, I have nothing to offer Nameera. She won't wait another year until I have fins again. It would be insulting to a Djinn.

You can't solve the riddle too quickly because it might offend the Djinn's intelligence. But you also can't take too long, as it's considered rude. They will have moved on, and the whole process will have to start over.

A giant waste of time.

We must find another way to fulfill the Djinn's desires, to get that damn lamp out of the ocean.

Perhaps there's another way out of this cursed body. Magic doesn't work on this body—not the way it should. I can't abandon it the same way I could leave any other human husk.

Zig is a Void.

I would have left his body and taken a witch. If I had magic, I could summon it. But no witch would trust me.

No witch would trust him either. My contacts have assured me they are looking for us.

There must be another way. I just can't see it.

Chapter 75

Dear Jensen

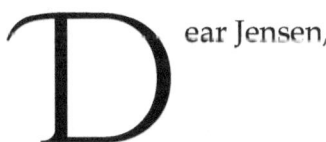ear Jensen,

I died today.

I died today, and Dagon brought me back to life. He gave up a chance at having a body of his own, rescued me, performed CPR, expelled the water from my lungs, and saved my life.

Do I trust the demon who saved me?

The mermaid?

Oh yeah, did I forget to mention that he's a mermaid?

I knew it, up here in my brain. But seeing it is a whole other story.

Dagon has a tail. After the six minutes were up, before my eyes, the tail shimmered away. Two legs were left in its place.

I need to save Zig.

I'll have to trust The Circle if I want to save him. The only person there I can trust right now is Azeltha.

She was my Sentinel once. Even if she doesn't understand, she'll listen.

That's all I need.

A chance to explain myself.

Scarlet

CHAPTER 76

AZELTHA

Dear Jensen,

The words appear in a journal of my own, mirroring Scarlet's.

I've always had my ways.

Do I trust the demon who saved me?

Oh, how the tides have changed.

Scarlet, what have you gotten yourself into?

CHAPTER 77

SCARLET

Every time I open my eyes, drifting in and out of sleep, Dagon is there, watching over me.

When daylight comes, I rouse enough to shoo him away, requesting a fresh pot of coffee and one of those Danishes he's always conjuring.

I shuffle into some clean clothes and follow my nose to a large cup of coffee on the counter next to a stack of Danishes and scrambled eggs.

"Thanks for this," I say, taking the cup and a plate of scrambled eggs. I add a lemon pastry to it and snag a fork.

"How are you feeling?" Dagon asks.

"I'm okay. Really," I say, maybe more for myself than for him.

"Good," he says, grabbing his cup of tea and a cherry Danish.

"I feel like I need to recap a little," I say. "We have no gift for Nameera. Correct?"

"Correct."

"Mermaids are murderers. Correct?"

"Not all of them. Some mermaids are actually quite lovely. They can use their siren song to save someone just as easily as they can use it to drown them. Sometimes it's a matter of perspective," Dagon says.

"Any chance we can woo one of them to our side?" I ask.

"Not likely, sorry," he says.

"You were a mermaid once. Doesn't that lend you any pull?" I ask.

"I was a sea god. There's a difference. Like I said, when people stopped believing," Dagon gives me a half smile. "Well, belief is everything."

"I wish I could trust all of this," I say, knowing full well that he was a mermaid last night, that I saw him with my own two eyes.

"What if I could show you?" Dagon says.

"How?" I ask hesitantly.

"With a kiss."

I spit out my coffee. "You're joking."

"No."

"I'm not falling for some kind of—" I shake my head, pushing this absurd thought away.

"I can't lie to you, Scarlet," Dagon reminds me. "We have a blood oath."

I take a bite of my pastry, another swig of my coffee, sit back in my chair, and look him in the eyes. "No tricks?"

Dagon grabs another Danish, this time an apple. "No tricks."

I take another sip, set my drink down, and stand. "Okay." My stomach knots the moment the word leaves my mouth.

Dagon stands and moves toward me slowly.

My heart thumps loudly in my chest.

Boom, boom, boom.

Dagon stands a foot from me.

Beads of sweat form on the back of my neck.

Six inches from me.

My hands start to tremble.

Our lips are two inches apart.

Shivers run up my spine.

One inch apart.

I think I'm going to vomit.

Our lips meet, and the world shifts and swirls around me like standing on the carousel at the carnival. Colors and faces blend into the background, some popping out more than others.

The past threads itself together with the present.

Confirming truths I wanted to ignore.

I tried to ignore.

Good truths.

Horrific truths.

Flashes of what was mingle with memories, building a more complex puzzle in my mind.

Pieces fit together for the first time, showing me a story of my life and what was.

What is.

What could be.

Our lips part.

I'm out of breath.

My stomach clenches with joy and sorrow.

I open my eyes, and Azeltha is standing next to us, arms crossed, watching.

CHAPTER 78

AZELTHA

S et your ego aside and save the Fountain at all costs,
Azeltha. That's what you signed up for.

When I see Scarlet Singer, hustler of demons and
humans alike, all that goes out the window.

"You're kissing the devil, Scarlet?" I spit my words at her,
ready to rip his throat out.

Zig be damned.

He's a small sacrifice in the grand scheme of this world.

All costs.

Dagon turns to me, hackles raised like the dog he is.

CHAPTER 79

SCARLET

"You're kissing the devil, Scarlet?" Azeltha's words are blades of ice moving through me, cutting every inch along the way.

"No, it's not like that," I say, but I shudder. "He's showing me the past. I—how? Where did you come from? How long have you been here? Is Marcus okay?" My words tumble out in a mishmash of brain fog and utter confusion.

"How could you forget who he is, Scarlet?" Azeltha says, never turning her back on Dagon.

"Stop," I say. "You can't kill him. Zig is still alive. You can't kill Zig. You can't. I'm saving him. I have a plan. Trust me."

"Stupid child. A plan?" Azeltha scoffs.

"You could trust me for once. I'm alive, aren't I?" I say, pleading with her.

"You've gotten lost along the way. Kissing that," Azeltha points at Dagon, who's taken a step back from me but hasn't moved otherwise. "You made a deal with a demon, Scarlet. I can't trust you or anything he does."

"How would you know that?" I say.

Azeltha doesn't answer.

"Have you been following me? Have you known where I am this whole time?" My voice breaks. "Gods, you're one to talk about trust. Have you been spying on me without once offering me help?"

Azeltha purses her lips.

"Fine, be that way." Tears threaten to spill over. "Shocker, I really can't trust anyone in this world. But you know what? I am a woman of my word, Azeltha. I need something from the bottom of the ocean. It's for a Djinn. If I get this item for her, I can save Zig."

"At what cost?" Azeltha asks.

Dagon harrumphs but doesn't speak.

Wise enough.

"Dagon gets a body of his own. No more human sacrifice. No more Zig sacrifice," I say.

"Did it ever occur to you that he can't leave Zig's body for a reason? Perhaps he's trapped there? Maybe it would be for the best to leave him in Zig's body," Azeltha says. "Have you thought for one moment about what Zig would want?"

"I don't care what Zig wants. I want death to stop falling at my hands. I want to know the truth about all of it. I want to understand. I need to know, Z. This is how we save Zig. I made a deal for his life," I say.

"Do you understand the price you'll pay?" Azeltha asks, looking from me to Dagon.

I look at her, and I muster a smile. "If I save him, and you, and Marcus, it doesn't matter."

CHAPTER 80

AZELTHA

It doesn't matter.

It does matter, stupid girl.

"It's a lamp at the bottom of the ocean, possibly with emerald adornments. But it's an empty magic lamp all the same," Scarlet says. "Probably."

I can't believe I'm even entertaining the idea. "That's not a lot to go on," I say.

"Were you there?" Scarlet asks.

I know she's talking about the Djinn, but I don't give her that. "I'm in a lot of places, child. What do you want from me?"

Scarlet's mouth settles into a hard line. She crosses her arms over her chest. "If you're not going to help us," she shakes her head. "Why did you come?"

Disappointment radiates from her.

"You," I say, pointing to Dagon, "over there."

He glowers down at me but obeys.

I walk to the ship's edge and feel for the object lost at sea. "Oculorum oriri oceanum hoc donum quaerunt," I cast, reveal what's hidden, rise from the ocean this gift they seek.

I feel the tug hidden from below. I've caught something in my magical net, and it slowly rises from depths unknown. I feel it tug against the ocean along the way, but when it reaches the surface, it rises out of the water and into my arms.

I hold the time-worn bottle in my palms and am overcome with anger. "Why shouldn't I destroy this? Or kill him on the spot? Give me a reason."

"Do it, witch," Dagon says.

I take a step toward him, and Scarlet steps between us. "Really? Is this what we've become?"

"You don't understand, Azeltha, and I want you to. I promise I will explain everything to you in time. I need you to trust me right now," Scarlet says, pleading with her eyes.

"You're asking me to trust him," I say. "That's something I'll never do."

"Stop with your empty threats, witch. The longer I'm in this body, the weaker Zig grows," Dagon says. "He will not survive to this moon."

"Don't lie to me. You don't speak," my words are a command.

"He can't lie to me," Scarlet says. "He's telling the truth."

"Did you ever ask him what happened to your dad? After he left your father to enter Zig?" I say.

Scarlet looks confused.

Had the thought never crossed her mind? "No, I suppose

you haven't. Don't be so blind, child. None of this can end well."

I didn't give Kelby a chance to make her choices, no matter how bad they were.

I promised I'd let Scarlet make her own. No matter how stupid they are.

I hand Scarlet the bottle. "I made choices for you once upon a time. I've regretted it every day of my existence since. I won't do it again. I just hope you know what you're doing."

Without another word, I leave.

I leave Scarlet to her own demise.

Zig to the demon's whims.

And the world, to her games.

Chapter 81

Scarlet

Azeltha is gone, and I suddenly feel cold and empty. All the hope I felt an hour ago has vanished with her.

Dagon is staring at the spot where she stood only moments ago.

I hold the jar in my hands, moving my fingers over it. Slime, earth, and age have not been kind to this bottle.

Dagon takes a step toward me.

"What happened to my dad?" I ask.

He stops, retracing his steps backward.

Evasive much.

"Dagon?"

"I didn't stay long enough to find out," he says.

"What is that supposed to mean?" I say, tears pricking my eyes again. A tightness forming in my throat. "Is he dead?"

Dagon shrugs his shoulders. "The opportunity was quick,

and I took it. I wasn't exactly invested in looking after your father. I'm sorry, Scarlet, I don't know."

"You don't know. Without any regard for him—you just let him die? You left him for dead?"

"I left him," Dagon says flatly. "I did not care at the time if he lived or died. All I cared about was you."

"If you cared about me at all, you would have made sure he lived," I say, thrusting the bottle into his chest. "Take your damn jar. Summon Nameera, take us wherever we need to go. Do whatever you need to do. Just leave whatever is left of Zig. I'm done. I'm done with you. I'm done with this. I'm done."

CHAPTER 82

MARCUS

Being patient has never been a gift of mine.

I pace the walls of Mundi, waiting for Azeltha to show herself, knowing there's not a damn thing I can do to help Scarlet.

I suffer in my waiting.

My mind spins stories of deceit, and I push the thoughts away.

I imagine her drowning, and my throat tightens.

There's no point in letting it take me to that dark place.

Azeltha appears.

"Is Scarlet alive? Did you find her?" I look around, half expecting Azeltha to have brought Scarlet with her. Realization dawns. "Where is she?"

"Sit down, niño," Azeltha says, moving slower than usual.

I don't sit. Instead, I watch her maneuver to a chair at my desk.

"Where's Scarlet," I ask again, my sanity slowly slipping away.

"She's alive," Azeltha says.

"How do you know?"

Azeltha waves her hand, and a glass of water appears. She takes her time answering my question. "Marcus, I need you to understand something."

"I think I understand more than I want to," I say.

"Sit down," Azeltha's words are a demand, not a request.

I sit.

"Scarlet is alive. But—"

"You've had me chasing ghosts for the last however many months when you knew exactly where she was this whole time?" I say, anger bubbling out.

I don't know how I didn't realize it before. How could I have been so blind?

Of course, Azeltha knew.

She knows everything.

I don't know how.

But she always knows.

"Would you have stopped looking for her if I told you I knew where she was, but I wasn't going to share that information with you?" Azeltha says.

"No," I say through clenched teeth.

"Well, there you go."

"That's not an answer," I say. "You can't logic this away. What aren't you telling me?"

Azeltha closes her eyes and nods her head, a slow defeat. "The Darkness has taken Zig."

I sit back and let her words sink in. A numbness moves through me.

I'm gutted.

I knew it was always a possibility.

But I'd hoped.

Naïveté at its best.

"Does Scarlet know?" I ask.

"Yes."

"Why didn't you tell me sooner? I would have—" I wipe away tears.

"You would have what, Marcus? Tell me, what would you have done to change things?"

"No matter the cost, I would have protected her," I say. "No matter the cost."

"That's what I've done," Azeltha says.

She doesn't meet my eyes.

"Tell me where she is," I demand.

"No."

"Tell me, Azeltha."

"It's not time."

"I'm done playing by your rules. All anyone does is lie to me. You bathe it in protection and call it for my own good. But that's crap, and you know it."

Azeltha meets my eyes.

"You knew this whole time, didn't you," I say.

Azeltha doesn't reply.

"You've taught me a lot, Azeltha. More than anything, you've shown me who I can't trust."

CHAPTER 83

DEAR JENSEN

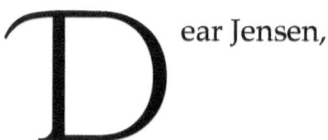ear Jensen,

I'M DONE WITH DAGON'S GAMES. I ASKED FOR ONE THING: TRUST.

I don't know how long Azeltha has been following us. Or if she even is? I'm not sure how she found us. Or if she's been tracking me all along?

It's really convenient that she showed up when she did. She just happened to know where I was and that I was dying? But not in time to save me.

It doesn't make sense.

She just left, too.

She didn't ask if I wanted to come. She didn't try to save me.

My heart aches at the betrayal.

Azeltha is high and mighty about right and wrong, but she didn't ask. She didn't listen. She never stopped to hear me out. If she read the journal with their stories, if she knew that the kiss was a stream of consciousness confirming memories from lifetimes ago—I don't think she would have been so quick to judge.

Maybe not.

Maybe I don't know her as well as I thought I did.

I don't know anything.

We got the gift for Nameera, and now we're headed back to her. It's the only way to save Zig.

I have to save Zig.

Everything I do has been with Zig in mind.

All of this can't be in vain.

That kiss.

It would take a book to explain everything I saw in that kiss.

I lived again in that kiss.

In Dagon's lips.

Is it possible to experience all of it and parts of life again? Even through his eyes, with a kiss?

I saw things I can't explain.

I have so many questions.

And Dad.

Is he alive?

Dead?

My heart hurts so much.

I'm tired of it hurting all the time.

I'm tired of pain being the norm.

Give me something else to live for.

Anything else because I'm running out of reasons.

Scarlet

CHAPTER 84

DAGON

We're nearly back to shore. Scarlet has avoided my eyes since Azeltha's departure.

I've wondered if we'd been followed. I've felt the prickle of watchful eyes for months.

It's been hours of silence. I know Scarlet's hungry, but she's too proud to ask for food or anything right now. I step into the galley and pull out a bottle of seltzer water. With a snap of my fingers, two large pizzas appear on the counter. I don't know what she's in the mood for, so I made both of her favorites.

I almost grab plates but decide that maybe having some peace-offering cookies would help. Another snap, and a platter of the ooiest, gooiest cookies fresh out of the oven appears.

Scarlet perks her head up.

"If you're hungry, there's some pizza," I say.

Scarlet's mouth twitches. "Help me to understand," she says.

So we're just going to skip the food and get right into this. Okay.

I take a breath and remember Ishara's words: Absolute honesty is the rawest form of giving up dominion over another person. "They knew I'd be evil from the beginning," I say. "It was always in the plan."

"You say that like there was some cosmic map predestined to make you so."

"There was. It didn't matter that the acts I'd done leading up to that decision were in service of light," I say.

"Oh—I thought," Scarlet starts to put the puzzle together. "Belief in a system, wherein whoever controls the system has the power."

I nod. "I was a benevolent leader. Good to my people. They never starved or paid a price for crimes they didn't commit. None of that matters now, and it didn't matter then. They didn't care about good and evil. They cared about power. This is what they made me into. They turned me into a beast and forced me to play the part."

"You act like they are puppet masters. You still made choices, Dagon. Don't forget that."

"I didn't choose to become a demon, Scarlet. Do you know why I seek you out, life after life? Over and over and over? Do you know why I torture both you and myself with this pitiful game we play?"

"Enlighten me," she says.

"Because you remember who I am. You are the only

person alive and breathing who has the ability to remember the real me. You remember Dagon before the uprising. Before I was a demon. No one else alive today can do that," my words hang in the air. "No one else will ever remember all I have done. The good still in me somewhere."

Scarlet takes my words in one by one. "Oh."

"You made me better. And they took you from me. Not just once, but repeatedly."

"What did you plan on doing after?" Scarlet asks.

"After?"

"Yeah, after. Like after you've swayed me to listen and believe you. What was your plan then?"

"I don't want you to be queen of hell if that's what you were thinking," I say.

"I wasn't," she waves me away.

I sigh. "You have your grace. You could heal us, Scarlet. We could live forever," I say. "My plan was to always be forgotten. You and me and forever without the prying human eyes. To fade into the distance like flowers on a clifftop. Enjoying the beauty from afar."

"Flowers on a clifftop?" she says.

"Untouched by human foils."

CHAPTER 85

SCARLET

We make land, but Dagon and I don't return to Pemberley. I could sleep for a month. Every part of me is exhausted, and I miss the comfort of a proper bed.

Instead, as if moving forward is an impossibility, we're back at the Dead Sea. We portaled after docking the boat.

Nameera waits for no man.

Perhaps when all of this is over, I can finally wash my hands of every conflicting and writhing emotion inside me.

I don't want to talk about things anymore or make more decisions.

There's a stirring inside of me for a monster. It doesn't matter where he's from. I can't shake the emotions and the memories.

When I think of this and see Zig's face, I feel two inches tall and ready to climb under a rock for eternity.

There was never a question in my mind about feelings.

There was never a doubt about who my heart belonged to.

But Dagon's words of late have struck a nerve that can't be numbed back into the darkness of before.

Before I knew too much.

Before the questions got complicated.

Before the answer became even more so.

Standing at the precipice of our future, Dagon drops the bottle into the Dead Sea.

Nothing happens.

I think back to the last time we summoned Nameera; I remember it took a while for her to respond.

We wait. I think of all the ways I have been betrayed. I think of trust.

When Nameera rises out of the water, she is something to be revered. Her translucence has taken on a rainbow tint this time.

"Dagon, you have returned. I'm surprised it didn't take you another three hundred years," Nameera says.

"I tried to waste more time, but alas," Dagon shrugs.

Nameera looks over her jar. Now that she's holding it, it's taken on a new shine, as if the bottle were brand new. "I wasn't sure you'd find it."

"If anything, I'm resourceful, Nameera; you should remember that," Dagon says.

"One wish, Dagon. Let's make it a good one, alright?" Nameera says, looking somehow bored of the conversation already.

"I wish for my own body back, leaving Zig intact and as he was before I entered him," Dagon says.

"You can ask for anything in the world, the universe having very few limitations on me, and that's what you ask for? You have always been sentimental, now haven't you," Nameera says.

Dagon clenches his jaw but doesn't speak.

"So be it. Your wish is my command, Dagon of this world, from once before and now. The body you speak of brought forth once more."

There's a lot of bright and blinding light, and the next thing I know, Nameera is gone.

Zig is passed out on the sand.

Dagon—I assume that's Dagon.

No.

I remember.

Oh, my stars, I remember.

That is Dagon.

Dagon, in his human form, stands across from me.

He's tall, with scruffy dark hair and olive skin. He's muscular and doesn't seem that much older than Zig. He has tattoos across his chest and arms. That's Dagon, just as I remember him.

Dagon has a body of his own.

Zig is safe.

CHAPTER 86

ZIG

Taking ownership of my body feels like emerging from a dark, residual place in my mind. Like being locked away in a little cage, suddenly free to move into the light, front and center again.

It's disorienting.

My thoughts are no longer muddled and sluggish.

My memory is clouded, though, like walking through a fog.

The last thing I remember was running with Scarlet. We were in Paris. And then... fragments come back to me. Memories of him inside me.

Of his thoughts.

I stand slowly, finding the use of my legs normal.

At least there's that.

Scarlet is watching him.

The body thief.

Dagon.

I feel my hands and note that he's left my rings on me. I summon The Circle without saying a word aloud. It shouldn't be too long until they track us.

"He doesn't need your body to walk in the world anymore, Scar; he's got his own," I say.

Scarlet spins and finds my eyes, her own tearing up at the sight of me.

"Come on, Scar, I don't look that bad, do I?" I tease.

She wipes away a tear. "I know. That was always the plan."

"Why, Scarlet? My life was never worth this. I would have saved yours at the cost of my own a thousandfold," I say.

"Yes, it is. So don't say that about my friend. I don't appreciate it," Scarlet says.

"You should have let me die," I say.

"Scarlet, The Circle is coming," Dagon says.

"But how?" Scarlet looks from me to Dagon.

"I summoned them," I say.

"We must go, Scarlet. We can't stay here. I won't invite a bloodbath," Dagon says.

"Don't go, Scarlet. You owe him nothing," I say, reaching for her.

She pulls away. "I owe him your life. I made a blood oath," Scarlet says. She moves toward me and cups my cheek. "You were always worth saving, Zig. The world needs you."

"No," I pull her hand down. "You made the oath with me. It's my body." I slap a hand to my chest. "Mine."

Scarlet shakes her head. "I can't trust that." I'm sorry. It's not—I can't let you die for me again, Zig."

"He's using you," I say. "Gods above, why can't you see that?"

"Everyone is," Scarlet says, calm. "The Circle has used me over and over for so many of my lives, Zig. They've tied me up and bled me for their convenience. They take what they want, tell me what they want, and lie to me when they want. I have never been seen as much more than property."

"What about Marcus and Azeltha?" I say, grasping for straws.

"Azeltha is the reason Kelby died. She's also why Marcus keeps looking for me, all the while having known where we are for months. I don't know what to believe anymore, Zig. All I know is that The Circle is no better." Scarlet sets her shoulders back, determined.

She's prepared for this conversation.

Probably played it out a thousand times in her head before we ever got this far.

"I know very little," Scarlet says. "But I know that I have to go." Scarlet wraps her arms around me and squeezes me tightly. "Give one of these to Marcus for me. I don't know if he'll ever understand. But I hope one day he does." Scarlet kisses me on the cheek and then lets me go.

Dagon turns his back to me, Scarlet follows him, and they walk into the darkness.

I wait, hoping she'll turn her head and look back.

Give me a sign that this is some kind of joke. That she's not really leaving with him.

But she doesn't.
I watch until she is gone.
Scarlet Singer is one with the darkness.
Scarlet Singer is no more.

Scarlet's story will continue.

MIRANDA LEVI

Stay updated with Miranda Levi's latest releases, author events, and the occasional free ebook sale. Sign up to be the first to know what's happening in her world of fiction!

ACKNOWLEDGMENTS

As I embark on any writing journey, I am surrounded by a tapestry of gratitude, woven with threads of unwavering support. My gratitude knows no bounds for the symphony of people who have played pivotal roles in bringing this book to life.

There are always many people to thank when writing a book. First, to my husband, thank you for being an endless source of support for all my writing endeavors. When I told him I would publish ten books this year, he might have gotten a little wide-eyed, but he still called me his badass author wife. His belief in me fuels my creative spirit, and for that, I am profoundly grateful.

To Jackson, there are never enough words to express my thanks for all you mean to me. You have been on this writing journey with me for many years, a steadfast companion pushing me to be a better person, writer, and editor. Your influence is immeasurable, and my gratitude is boundless.

To Angie and Melanie, my cheerleaders, and constant support—you ladies are my reason, not just my family. Your encouragement has been a steady heartbeat, echoing in the background of my creative process. Thank you for being the pillars upon which I lean.

Yet, amidst all these expressions of gratitude, the most profound thanks belong to you, the readers. Without you, this book might have remained a silent echo within the confines of my computer. Your patience over the past year as Scarlet, Dagon, Zig, and Marcus's continued story took shape means more than words can convey. Thank you for not only waiting but also for asking and begging for more. I sincerely hope this offering satisfies your Fountain of Youth cravings, at least for a time.

MIRANDA LEVI

Fountain of Youth Trilogy book 3
by Miranda Levi.

CHAPTER 1

AGNES

With a crack, the world shatters—not the literal stones underfoot, but something deeper. A split through the heart of my reality. I feel it first in my chest, a fissure of soul.

The night is ink-thick and heavy with silence. Around me, cloaked figures gather. Their faces are hidden, but their horns gleam like bone. The torches in their hands flicker against the mist, casting phantoms that dance and leer. Smoke curls in a language of its own.

They believe this is an end.

But I know better.

This is only the beginning.

The stars above are witnesses—no, accomplices—scattered across the sky like shards from some great celestial mirror.

I kneel, palms pressed to the damp earth, and whisper my

final devotion. "Dagon," I breathe, and the name carries power. It trembles against the stones.

He steps from the dark like he's always belonged there—an outline first, then flesh and shadow twined. Dagon, my tether and undoing. A god cloaked in wrath and sorrow.

His voice is a storm swallowed in gravel. "Say the word and I will take you from this place."

I rise to my feet. We're so close our breath becomes shared air. His presence curls around me, ancient and hungry, but softened at the edges when he speaks.

"Do not save me," I whisper, my fingers brushing his. "Not this time."

"You ask too much," he growls. "They will chase us beyond the veil, Agnes. You know what they fear—what we are."

"Let them chase," I say. "Let them burn their feet on the path we carved. But it is not for me to be spared."

Dagon's expression twists into something pained, and for once, mortal. "You would make me live without you again?"

"I would make you find me," I whisper. "In another life. Another time."

He trembles like a fault line about to break. "I will burn this world to ash before I forget you."

Our kiss is not sweet. It's carved from centuries, stitched from salt and shadow. It tastes like sorrow and fury, but also something achingly tender. The world pauses for that kiss.

Then the circle closes.

And then, I wake.

I gasp like I've surfaced from the bottom of the ocean.

The bed beneath me is too soft. The air is too still. The silence is *wrong*. I jolt upright, heart thrashing, as if the fire's still burning beneath my skin.

The dream—vision—memory—whatever it is, it clings like salt on my tongue. The kiss, the flames, the promise.

I blink up at the ceiling—smooth plaster, unfamiliar, high and sloped like the bones of an old cathedral. A faded mural of stars arcs across it. Not the cracked ceiling of my room at Mundi.

But I remember now.

Dagon didn't say where exactly we were, only that it was *safe*. I'm ninety percent sure that were at Pemberly.

But nothing feels safe when your past lives are haunting you like a ghost pressing warm lips to yours.

The sheets are twisted around my legs. I press a hand to my chest, but it doesn't steady anything. The ache is still there. The memory of Agnes's final breath still wrapped around my lungs.

He's already watching.

Of course he is.

Dagon sits in the armchair by the fire, shirtless, shadows curling around his spine like they belong there. His eyes—ancient, knowing, *mine*—glow faintly in the low light.

He doesn't ask what I saw.

He already knows.

I wrap the blanket tighter around my body, like I'm suddenly cold. "It was her again."

He hums softly. "It's always her."

"She burned for you," I whisper. "She *chose* to burn."

His jaw clenches, a flicker of guilt crossing his face. "She thought it would break the cycle."

"And did it?" I ask.

He doesn't answer. He doesn't have to.

I rub my hands over my arms, trying to ground myself in this version of reality. "How long was I under?"

"A few hours. You said my name before you went still."

"Dagon?"

He nods once.

Not Zig. Not the boy I used to know.

He's real now. Made of flesh and storm and the pieces I remember too well.

I glance toward the window. The curtains are drawn, but faint light bleeds through them. Not sunlight. Moonlight. Blue and silver.

Cold.

"I felt everything," I say. "Like I was there. Like I *was* her."

"You *were* her." His voice is too calm. "You still are."

"Then why do I feel like I'm betraying myself?"

He rises slowly, graceful as the tide, and crosses the room. When he kneels in front of me, I swear I feel the ocean in his skin—salt, sorrow, power coiled and waiting.

"You're not betraying anyone," he says. "You're remembering. That's different."

My hands tremble. He takes them gently, fingers rough and reverent.

"Every lifetime," he murmurs, "you come back to me."

"Every lifetime," I whisper back, "I die for you."

He doesn't flinch. Doesn't apologize. Doesn't lie.

"That's what terrifies me the most," I say. "That I'll do it again."

Dagon lifts one of my hands to his lips. The kiss is soft. Not possessive. Not demanding. Just a promise: *I'm still here.*

"And if this time," he says carefully, "we rewrite the ending?"

I look at him. The man. The god. The monster.

The only constant in every version of me.

"I don't know if we're capable of endings that don't burn."

Dagon's smile is slow, sad, and strangely beautiful. "Then let's learn to rise from the ash together."

I want to believe him.

But I'm still tasting smoke.

www.MirandaLevi.com

www.ingramcontent.com/pod-product-compliance
Lightning Source LLC
Chambersburg PA
CBHW032206030726
47494CB00020B/633